THE DOUBLE

CLINT WESTGARD

ALSO BY CLINT WESTGARD

Unspeakable Rites: An Alkemya Novella

The Shadow Men:

    Realm of Shadows

    Council of Shadows

    Dance of Shadows

The Sojourners Cycle:

    The Forgotten

    The Apostate

    The Acolyte

    The Double

    The Sojourner (forthcoming)

The Maleficio Chronicles

Trials of the Minotaur

The Farthest Reaches: A Collection

Published by Lost Quarter Books
www.lostquarterbooks.com

This edition 2018

ISBN: 978-1-928035-44-2

For Mary Shelley

CONTENTS

PROLOGUE   1

ONE   THE GRAND REGENT'S TOWER   4

TWO   A FAITH CONFIRMED   59

THREE   AFTEREFFECTS   95

FOUR   A FAITH BETRAYED   161

PROLOGUE

I lie, floating, in darkness and absence. There is no light, not even a hint of its presence. It feels as though I have just awoken from a deep slumber and am fighting to open my eyes, but they resist, wanting to stay in this comforting nothing for a little longer. Time is short, though—I feel that too, deeply—and I must arise.

This is a place I inhabit, though what sort of place I am unsure. A stasis chamber, perhaps, though only the Travelers use those. Am I now somehow in their possession? I struggle to recall what has happened, what events led me to here. There is no clarity in my thoughts. An assortment of memories without connection flicker by but do not adhere to me. They are not mine. Or they are, but I am many. No longer one.

How can this be? It cannot persist. Someone must rule; someone must be in command.

And it must be me. That is the urgency I feel. I do not know what will happen if I remain here. Perhaps I will wither to nothing, like a muscle unused. Or I will be subsumed beneath the cacophony of memory and voices until I forget which one I am. Which me is me. Even now I am not certain.

But I am not quite ready to leave this darkness. I cannot find the strength to move. There is both comfort and terror here. Comfort, in the hope that I might dissolve into this nothingness. The endless voices and memories might dissipate and I can be free. Terror at who I might be, at the many who might assert themselves, or the possibility that none will, that I will forever be trapped in this struggle.

A distant rumble reaches my ears, a cataclysm in some other universe from long ago, whose aftershock is only now reaching this place and this time. I tremble in response, drawn a little further into awareness. The contours of this place are now more apparent to me, their shape and hue made evident by the aftershocks. There is a place in the far distance that I can almost see where the void ceases and something else begins.

A swirling darkness resides there, absent of light and movement, or time and space itself. An absolute nothingness. Gradually I become aware that my apparent stillness is a lie and I am being drawn toward it, inching ever closer. At first, I struggle and fight against it, but its pull is as inexorable as any planet's gravity. Perhaps this is my ultimate fate. To be trapped in this timeless present, forever lost and forever aware.

As I am drawn nearer, I see the edges of this voidless abyss. It is like the swirling rush of a whirlpool gone still. At the center lies another kind of darkness, more absolute than even the one I inhabit now. Beyond that darkness lies something else. I cannot sense it, but I know it is there and I know there is path through this still whirlpool, if I can navigate. And somewhere, in that beyond, there is a light. Green and blue, repeating flashes, like a beacon left to show me the way.

ONE:

THE GRAND REGENT'S TOWER

1

The Grand Regent sits upon his throne, surveying the audience room atop De Gofroy's tower. I stand at his side, as expressionless as I can manage, though I am suppressing a grin of delight. At long last, I have returned to my rightful place. A sub-Regent of the Watchers' Order. A servant to the Grand Regent. A shield against all those who would stand against the faith.

The Grand Regent studies those gathered before him, casting his eyes from one face to the next, as though seeking to penetrate whatever walls they have built up to keep their secrets from the faith. That is against the Protocols, as we all know. What his gaze tells them is that he will see them revealed. And my presence says that, if he is unable to, the Order shall do the work for him.

Everyone here knows what that means, some of us only too well. I see Morris Loverne, that traitor, now rendered compliant, standing alert and stiff at the back of the audience chamber, ready to act should the need arise. It will not. His remaining loyalists within the Church have been arrested and subjected to the Acolyte's ministrations. The rest are scattered to the winds. But with what he has already revealed and what I know, we shall find the rest

5

soon enough. Laila Johar, the companion of my mind and enemy of the faith, has been overthrown and banished. I rule this flesh now. She is but a distant voice I barely hear. I have choked the life from her.

It still feels strange to stand here in my own body, to have it respond to my thoughts, to think what I wish to think, and to act as I see fit. I want to luxuriate in the glorious sensation of it all. To be me again, to be truly me. There are the memories the Acolytes stole from me, but that is a nuisance, nothing more. They can be restored, surely, and Laila removed from within me. I will ask the Grand Regent when the time is right.

For now I watch him, savoring my moment of triumph. Our triumph. At length, he stands and begins to speak.

"I am here to welcome back a faithful vessel to the Church and the Watchers' Order. David Aeida." He pauses to turn to me, and I bow to him. An ironic smile crosses his lips. "David Aeida has been a faithful vessel. More than any of you will ever know. Perhaps more than even he himself is aware.

"He has returned to us after some time abroad." Here he offers a small gesture with his fingers and another ironic smile. "Much has changed since he left and he has learned much about our enemies, as he has told me a little. I will learn more from him in the coming days, I am sure, for David has much to share."

He rewards me with a warm smile. I am unable to stop myself from beaming. Looking out over the assembled, I am met by blank, unwavering stares. The grim, expressionless visages of those gathered unsettles me. How many here have been brought before the Acolytes to be returned to the ranks of the faithful? Morris Loverne for one. Myself for another.

I scan the faces, looking for anyone familiar. There are a few of the loyalist High Regents—at least they were High Regents when I was last involved in the Order—and surely they would be left untouched by the Acolytes, or else they would have been removed from their positions. The Grand Regent cannot keep those he does not trust so near and in such influential positions in the Hierarchy. Their unchanging stares and similar expressions all leave me with a sense of deep disquiet.

The Grand Regent pauses, considering his next words. "The last years have been difficult for the faith. De Gofroy's vision was almost vanquished. I have fought to ensure that the quest for the one true universe can continue, and now I feel we are closer than ever to achieving it. Many have fallen in the pursuit of that quest, and we should remember them now."

He looks to the ceiling solemnly, intoning a brief prayer, his words so quiet that I cannot make them out. When he is finished, he turns back to the assembled. "And make no mistake, we must stay on our guard. The Order has done wonderful work in rooting out the Society agents in our midst, to say nothing of the apostates who would pervert De Gofroy's words. We are so near to triumphing over them both. I can feel it in my soul.

"David Aeida is central to that effort," he says, as if suddenly recalling that I am present, standing beside him. "There will be difficult days that lie ahead, for all of us. But now we are on the path to reuniting our fragmented beings with our true selves—to be Regents no more—I feel certain these sacrifices will all be worth it. We shall save not only ourselves, but billions across untold universes. Never forget that what we do, all we sacrifice, is for them."

The Grand Regent nods, a dismissal of sorts. Those assembled bow as one being and shuffle out the door under the watchful gaze of Morris Loverne, who resumes his post outside the audience chamber door. The Grand Regent turns to me, the ironic smile returning to his face.

"We have much to discuss, David Aeida. Much to discuss. Where would you have us begin?"

I swallow and try to meet the Grand Regent's gaze, but am unable to. The sharp blue of his eyes seems to cut through my defenses, piercing right to the center of me. Laila was never so intimidated as I am, seeing him for what he is. A leader of the faith, but a man, nonetheless, and fallible in the way all of us are. It is that second I have difficulties reconciling myself with. She loved him and was loved by him, and I have seen those memories from a distance when my mind was not my own.

He is not to be trusted, that much I know and need to keep reminding myself. He will use me as he sees fit, casting me aside or sending me to my doom, telling himself it is for the greater good of the faith. He may not even be wrong. I have my own ends to see to, though, and I will need to protect myself. So there are some things that I have seen in Laila's mind that will stay mine, at least for now.

The Grand Regent is waiting for me to speak. I hesitate, unsure what tack to use, ultimately deciding to throw caution to the wind and ask for what I truly desire. "Now that I have returned and proven my absolute loyalty to the faith, I would like to have her removed from my mind." I will not say her name.

His expression does not change but his eyes harden at my words. "That is impossible, I'm afraid."

"Grand Regent, I know the Acolytes can do this. And it must be done. So long as she remains within me, I am a danger to you."

He frowns, sitting down upon his throne and resting his chin upon his hand. "You told me you had vanquished her."

"I have," I say. "But can you afford to risk me being wrong? I know what her thoughts about you and the faith are. She will stop at nothing to destroy you."

The Grand Regent's face darkens, and I fear I have gone too far. He never did like to hear how Laila truly felt about him, even when she told him herself. It is important for him to believe that, in spite of all that has happened, all that has come between them, she still loves him.

"I think you misjudge her. You do not know her as I do," the Grand Regent says in a wistful voice.

I am unable to stop myself from recalling the moment when I asserted myself completely over Laila, when her own body—and whatever was in its mind—emerged from behind this very throne to derail her sense of herself. What else does the Grand Regent do with that compliant flesh? I suspect the answer is entirely unpleasant, though I am hardly one to cast aspersions in that regard.

"But it doesn't matter, even if you're right," he continues, musing more to himself than to me. "We need access to Laila's memories in a controlled environment, now that we know she has been working with the Seeker for as long as she has."

I want to interrupt and say this was a recent development, that her earlier dalliance with the Society was more a dalliance with Ana than anything else, at least from what I have witnessed. Her current arrangement was a forced one; she was given no choice. But I can sense he does not wish to be interrupted and that such nuances will only make him less likely to accede to my wishes. I need him on my side and believing in me, if I am to convince him that removing Laila is a benefit to us all.

Most importantly, I cannot let him know that Laila is gone, vanished from my mind. At least for the moment. I am not fool enough to believe that she is gone for good. That is why I want her removed, so there can be no doubt. This body is mine.

When I banished her, it was not like when she wrested control from me and the blank construct the Acolytes built in this body. Throughout all of that I had been more or less aware, though powerless to do anything, unable to take command of my body for more than a few fleeting moments. Now she is gone, utterly, and I cannot see any of her thoughts and memories, as she could see mine and I hers when we were intermingled. All I have is what I can remember of what I have seen, which will have to be enough.

"There are things she knows that we will need to know." The Grand Regent nods, as though to assure himself this is correct. "Besides, I have the perfect guard against her return. Someone who will know beyond any doubt if she is mounting an effort to replace you."

He smiles, an infuriating smile. I do not need to be told who it is to know. Glancing over his shoulder, he calls to someone in the rooms behind the audience chamber.

"You may show yourself now."

I watch, alternating between fury and despair, as Meredith emerges to stand beside the throne.

2

I am assigned quarters in the tower, down the hall from the Grand Regent's rooms. Meredith has a room next to mine. There are probably cameras or listening devices installed so that she can keep careful observation on me, but I make no move to disturb them. Let her watch. It will be torture for her, as she hopes against hope for any sign of Laila's return.

At my first sight of her, I was unable to contain myself. "You would set her to watch over me?" I said to the Grand Regent. "After what she did in the other universe. She wants Laila to return."

Meredith offered only a cool smile in response, her face unreadable.

The Grand Regent shook his head. "I understand your angst, but Meredith has long been a faithful vessel."

Again I failed to control my emotions. "How can you say that? She betrays everyone who trusts her. Osahi. Her. You. Why give her the chance to do so again?"

"I understand your doubt," the Grand Regent said, rising to his feet. The audience was over and I was being dismissed. "But you have not been so loyal yourself, David Aeida. Meredith has her part to play. As do you. These

11

matters will become clear in time."

I pace about my room restless with anger as I recall that conversation. It is dangerous to keep Meredith around. Laila is drawn to her and may awaken if she is near. As confident as I am that I have vanquished her, and as absent as she is now, I cannot let my guard down. She can return. It has happened before, after all. How many times, only Meredith knows.

That is not the only reason she is a problem for me. If she has the Grand Regent's ear, it will mean trouble in the long run. She will not want Laila removed or destroyed. Even if we can somehow find common ground, I cannot work with her; she cannot be trusted. So I will have to remove her somehow. The Grand Regent seems set on the matter, and she is clever, so it will be a difficult task, but one I will have to succeed at if I am to get what I want.

I put those thoughts reluctantly aside for the moment and decide to leave my quarters. There is nothing to be done today about any of those problems. My more immediate concern is to become familiar again with my surroundings. I have never been in the Grand Regent's tower before; as a sub-Regent I was never allowed to leave my universe. Laila was, but much has changed since she was last here, and my recollections of her memories are necessarily limited.

The audience chamber with its throne and Mayan symbols has grown only more ostentatious since she left. The whole floor has been similarly refurbished with fantastic artifacts and tapestries lining the walls and marble flooring running down each hallway. Some of the rooms have been rebuilt and repurposed, but the overall layout remains much the same, with the elevator banks at the center of the building, and rooms spreading out on either side.

My quarters are on the far side of the elevators from the Grand Regents rooms, and I follow the corridor away from the audience chamber and find myself at a small alcove with a window overlooking the entire Church campus. It is where Laila had her encounter with Frederik and where she truly realized the depths of what had been done to De Gofroy's son by the Acolytes. One of them, the scarred man who I had also encountered, emerged and took Frederik away into one of the rooms along the corridor.

My room, I realize. And Meredith's is the Acolyte's, no doubt. Which means my position here is much more circumscribed than I had imagined, and certainly not as the Grand Regent intimated. What does he want me for? Perhaps he wants to observe me for a time before having the Acolytes restore the Joseph Aurellano cipher and tamp my mind, so that I disappear again along with Laila. That was inherently unstable, though, as even the Grand Regent must realize now. If he doesn't, I will have to make him.

Meredith appears beside me, startling me from these disquieting thoughts. She studies me as though she can see to the depths of me where Laila resides, which only makes me more uncomfortable.

"Adjusting to your new surroundings, Aeida?" she says in an accusing tone.

I wince and smile. "It's all new to me."

"No, it isn't," she says.

"I'm not going to allow her to return. This is my body."

"That is not for you to decide." She pauses, a terrible smile coming over her face. "You are a faithful vessel. Nothing more."

I clench my fists in rage and choke back the temptation to throw her words back in her face. We both know how circumscribed our existences are now that we have been shown to be lacking in the eyes of the Grand Regent. Meredith will watch me, and someone will observe her, and the Acolytes will stand ready to be summoned to deal with any betrayals of the faith.

"Of course," I force myself to say. "I serve the Grand

Regent and the Order."

"Good. He has summoned you. Are you ready?"

Ready for what? I want to say, but I simply nod and allow her to lead me back to the audience chamber. She takes me through that room to the Grand Regent's quarters, which lie behind them. He is sitting at a dark wooded table in an antique chair with baroque carved Mayan symbols atop its back. *Another throne.* That bitter thought vanishes as I take in who is sitting across from him. Toma Osahi.

I stumble where I stand and have to reach out to clutch the back of the nearest chair—ornately carved as well—to stop myself from falling. Meredith reaches out a hand to support me, but I shrug her off. The Grand Regent watches with what appears to be curiosity and gestures for us to sit. I do, with relief that I am unable to disguise, my head still buzzing and light, my eyes struggling to regain their focus.

Perhaps it is simply the exhaustion of the past few days. The crossings took their toll—that was what, in part, allowed me to overthrow Laila. As did the debriefings with the Grand Regent and the Order that followed. The shock of seeing Meredith and realizing the terrible precariousness of my situation, along with this new surprise, is simply too much.

It is not Laila attempting to return. That is what I tell myself, anyway. I reach into the darkness where once Laila was, but there is no sign of her. She has not returned.

"I should have known," I manage to say, my words slurring a little. That frightens me, and my hands clench my legs to try to restore my balance, which seems to be eroding by the second.

Osahi laughs. He is wearing a peacock-blue jacket and what I can only describe as a pirate shirt, looking every bit the dandy again now that his exile is over. "I'm surprised Laila didn't suspect it. She had a nose for these sorts of things."

I shake my head. "She did wonder. But she was not herself."

In truth, she did not understand Osahi. She thought him an idealist, an adherent of De Gofroy's vision that Molijc had perverted. Osahi may believe that as well, but he is fundamentally a creature of the Protectorship and the Hierarchy. For him, the Church is ultimately the faith; the Protocols and the one universe and our true selves are all esoterica. A Grand Regent may go astray, but the Church will ultimately remain true to the faith. It will stand. And Osahi, above all, wants to be there to ensure that it does.

"I suppose not," Osahi says, studying me closely, wondering, no doubt, if any of Laila remains awake within me. I return his smile as best I can.

The Grand Regent frowns, clearly displeased with the direction the conversation has gone. "As David Aeida has returned to the faith, so has High Regent Osahi," he says, as though he is still speaking to the assembled in the audience room. "The High Regent has long been a faithful servant of the Protectors, guarding the faith against the incursions of the Society of Travelers. His work in that regard has not been forgotten, and it will continue again now that he has returned to the fold."

What deal did Osahi cut with the Grand Regent? I wonder. I am the prize he traded, but what does he expect in return? It cannot simply be restoration of his role in the Church Hierarchy. He was High Regent before, and it offered no protection against the Watchers' Order or the Acolytes. Does he still oppose what the Order is doing, or is he happy to let it continue so long as his people are excluded?

The thought of his people makes me wonder what happened to Suon. I put the question to Osahi.

"She is no concern of yours," Osahi says, menace in his voice.

It is hard to know what he means by that, but that is in part because I remain uncertain of Suon's own attitude.

Somehow Osahi learned that Laila resided in this body, and Suon is the most likely suspect. Yet, by her own words, she wanted to abandon the faith and for Laila to go with her, to say nothing of her declaration of love. Were those words the truth or the duplicity of an agent of Osahi? Laila believed it was the latter.

As for me, I realize it no longer matters. Suon is of no consequence now.

"Indeed," the Grand Regent says, his annoyance at my interruption evident. "The three of you will begin working on a special task, the importance of which I cannot stress enough. It breaks my heart to say it, but David Aeida has made it clear that Laila was an agent of the Seeker and worked for the Society. Morris Loverne, her most trusted lieutenant, was similarly an agent of the Travelers. We must find out how deep this terrible sickness has penetrated into the heart of the Church. We must root it out. We must cure our faith."

He pauses to gather his breath, his face flushed with anger, and looks from Osahi to Meredith and to me. "You three will do this. You will use Laila's memories and your assets in the Society and you will find out how deep this goes."

"We will not fail," Osahi says with authority. "I know how to find out the truth of things."

The last is uttered as a threat, whether at me or Meredith—or the Grand Regent himself—I am not certain. I do not have time to ponder that, for the Grand Regent stands up from his chair and looks us over. We are dismissed. The three of us make our way out through the audience chamber and out into the corridor, no one speaking.

I pause for a moment by the doorway to see if any of the others have anything to say about what has just occurred. Meredith brushes past me and heads to her room, not looking at either of us. Osahi grins and gets into the elevator, his eyes intent on mine until the door closes and takes him away.

I am left alone and disquieted, unsure how next to proceed. Osahi has some game that he is playing, but is the Grand Regent aware of what it is? Meredith is a prisoner in this, as am I, neither of us willing or able to break with the Grand Regent. We are trapped and will do what we can to avoid the Acolytes being summoned to do their work.

Most confusing of all is the great task the Grand Regent has left to us. I have told him all there is to know about Laila's involvement with the Seekers. There is nothing left to be discovered there, in part because her memories are lost to me. All I know is what I have seen.

But it is of little consequence. Her network is crippled. The Order will have learned all they needed to know about it from Morris Loverne. Even if there is something still to be discovered, that is easily left to the Watchers. Better left to them in fact, given the doubts the Grand Regent must have about all of us.

So why hasn't he? And where is my old mentor Lasinha in all this? He knew not to trust Osahi and Meredith and Laila. His absence at this time of alliances with old enemies is very strange.

3

The next days pass without incident. I do not see the Grand Regent, but Morris, or what remains of him, tells me he is in his quarters and does not wish to be disturbed. I spend most of those first days haunting the corridor running from my room past the elevators to the Grand Regent's chambers, waiting to see who will emerge and who will go in. No one does. The only person I see is the half-Morris who stands stiff and unmoving throughout the day.

Why does the Grand Regent trust his security to a half-thing, one of the Acolytes' creatures? They are inherently unstable. That has been both my observation and my experience. How many times did the Order bring someone back to the compound in the other universe for the Acolytes to work on because the effects of their procedure were wearing off, or growing deleterious? Perhaps they have perfected their procedures in the time I was exiled, but I suspect not.

The absence of any visitors of import, as well as the glaring lack of activity by the Grand Regent—surely he must have official duties to attend to—only grow more disturbing the longer I remain, so I decide to leave to see if

I can find Lasinha. Meredith is nowhere to be found—I presume she is still in her quarters—and I decide if she wants to follow me, she can.

I take the elevator to the main floor of the tower and step outside, and am startled by the crisp air. It is spring, or fall, I cannot tell. The grass is brown and the trees have no leaves upon them. It is barely above freezing and the wind has a sharp edge to it. I am too used to Vancouver, where a bright sun and cloudless day, as there is here now, portend warm weather.

Perhaps that explains why I see no one on any of the pathways stretching between the buildings. I have emerged on the east side of the tower and can see the Protector's House and the Acolytes' building, among others. On the other side will be the dormitories for the Regents, which I passed under on my way to the tower to confront the Grand Regent. Still, the absence of any sign of humanity, even members of the Order or Protectors who might be keeping an eye on me, fills me with unease.

The wind gusts and swirls, stirring up a fine grit that works its way into my eyes. I scurry up the hill toward the Protector's House. Lasinha's office was once here, and perhaps it still is. I need to find him. He is the only one I can truly trust, though he left me to this fate. But that was not his doing; he had no choice in the matter. It was my own foolishness, which left the Grand Regent with no choice but to act.

My footsteps echo down the empty corridor as I make my way toward his old office on the main floor of the building. All the doors I pass are closed and the abandoned hallways feel both cold and stuffy, as if the air has ceased to move. It is all so strange, and my sense of foreboding, already deep, only grows the farther along I go. Though it seems impossible, it appears there is no one at all in the building.

When I arrive at Lasinha's office, I can hear typing on a keyboard behind the door and relief floods through me. I knock and hear a familiar voice. "It's open."

I throw the door open and step inside to level an accusing glare at Suon, who raises an eyebrow in mild surprise. "What are you doing here?" I say.

"I could ask the same of you," she says mildly, turning back to the screen. A few mouse clicks indicate that she is clearing whatever is on it before I can step around the desk and see it.

"This is Lasinha's office," I say. "You have no right to be here."

"It *was* Lasinha's office," she says, but does not explain what she means.

"Where is he?" I say, before I can stop myself.

"I don't know. He's not here. You should ask the Grand Regent."

"I will," I say. "There's a lot I need to speak to him about. I know Osahi is up to something. The Grand Regent is wrong to trust him."

Suon laughs bitterly. "I think you'll discover the Grand Regent doesn't trust anyone. I'm surprised you don't know that already. As for Toma, well, he sees an opportunity."

"What sort of opportunity?"

"That you will see in due time, David Aeida," Osahi says from behind me.

In spite of myself, I jump in surprise and whirl around to face him. How the hell did he come down the hallway without my realizing it?

"What is that supposed to mean?" I say, trying for a bravado I don't feel.

Osahi ignores me and looks to Suon, a question in his eyes. She shakes her head.

"Nothing yet."

He frowns. "Well. Keep trying. Something will turn up."

"We are supposed to be looking for Society agents," I say. "Or do you so soon forget what the Grand Regent asked of us?"

Osahi gives me a mirthless smile. "Molijc sees Travelers' shadows wherever he looks, without ever realizing that his greatest enemies lie closest at hand. Like you, for instance. Or what lies within, anyway."

"She was in league with the Society."

Osahi shakes his head. "I think we both know that's not the case. Just as we both know there is no more water to be wrung from her memories."

It is more the case than he can know, but I don't say that to Osahi. If the Grand Regent realizes that Laila is gone, he might ask the Acolytes to try to bring her back to pursue this mad investigation. I cannot risk that happening and losing control to her again.

"I have important things to do," Osahi continues, looking at Suon. "And I do not intend to waste my time with wild chases that will lead nowhere. But you may run and tell the Grand Regent that I am being disobedient. Be careful, though. He is mistrustful of messengers. Among many other things."

I glare at Osahi and Suon, shifting my gaze from one to the other. They both look at me placidly, as though I am a nuisance to be tolerated, but ultimately of no consequence.

"If we are finished?" Osahi says pointedly, gesturing toward the door.

I try to think of something more to say, but everything sounds weak to my ears, and I abandon the attempt and walk out the door. It is closed behind me, and I can hear Osahi speaking to Suon in a hushed voice, but cannot make out any words. I hesitate, wondering if it is worth the effort to try to hear what they are saying, before abandoning the idea and walking away.

After thinking about exploring the campus further, I abandon the idea and return to my quarters. The prospect of empty and abandoned Church buildings is too much for me to bear at the moment. What has become of the faith during my exile? It seems worse than even Laila imagined, and she is an apostate. Where is the Order? Where is

Lasinha? He would not allow the faith to crumble as it appears to have.

We are at war, of course—both within the faith and without—and with war comes casualties and sacrifices. The Grand Regent seems unconcerned and talks of things being revealed in due time. I shall just have to try to earn his confidence, so that he might reveal what plans he and Lasinha have in place to restore the glory of the Church. For the campus now seems desolate, the faithful absent, and predators like Osahi are on the march, ready to seize what little flesh yet remains upon the carcass.

I feel as though I should be doing something to fight this; I am a sub-Regent of the Order, after all. But it is impossible for me to determine what that might be, given how little I know of what is actually going on. The Grand Regent has given me a task, an important one in his words. Neither Meredith nor Osahi appear to be taking it seriously, which is both a relief and a concern. It means they believe there is nothing more to be discovered about Laila and are both working on their own schemes.

That is what the Grand Regent should be concerning himself with. It is what I should be telling him, but I cannot. He may turn me over to the Acolytes if he sees no use to me. So long as he thinks I can provide access to Laila, he will keep me around. It feels terrible to mislead him, but I tell myself it is necessary. And he will not be harmed by it. On the contrary, I may be able to better protect him from those who would lead him astray.

The Order, with their tentacles reaching throughout the faith and beyond, should keep him well informed as well. Their reports to the Grand Regent will eventually reveal the truth of what Osahi and Meredith are about. Once I helped write those reports. Now I am not trusted, and I am not privy to the inner workings of the faith or the Order. Then, it was easier to know what was needed to protect the faith. Now, I am lost and left with only memories of those days.

They beckon to me, those memories. I long to go there and leave this miserable present, where I am nothing and the faith seems reduced and somehow pathetic. How long did I yearn to come to this campus? Now that I am finally here, sitting at the feet of the Grand Regent, an absence touches everything. The Church has the feeling of a dead thing, still shuffling along, its motion carrying it forward even after its demise. It is not true, I tell myself, but it is the unease that worries at me every waking moment.

Far better to abandon the present, pitiful as it is, and the uncertain future, where I may never find myself truly free of the specter of Laila in my thoughts. Or the Acolytes' suppressants and tamps. Better to return to when I was master of my own fate, the undisputed ruler of my thoughts, before everything went so wrong. I can lose myself there.

Why return? Why should I not dwell there? It is my place, after all, though the places where the memories have gone haunt me. I can still feel the outlines of where they should be—my mother's face, childhood friends and incidents, so much is lost—like an amputated limb. But there is much still there, much to embrace. After being banished for so long, my memories left for Laila to rummage through at her whim, it is wonderful to be able to remember what once was. To feel as I once did, whole and complete.

I lie down upon the bed in my quarters and close my eyes. The Grand Regent's bidding can wait. The faith can wait. I will remember.

4

From my car seat, where I sat ostensibly studying the screen of my cell phone, I watched as Meredith crossed the street in front of me amidst a throng of other passersby. She did not notice me, but I was always skilled at making sure I went unnoticed, and she did not think anyone would be watching her in that universe. Of course, it was my universe, the Order's universe. But then, she knew that too.

Once she was across the crosswalk, she turned and crossed the street she had been walking down to the far side of the intersection I was watching. I did not have to watch where she was going then, I knew for a certainty, but still, I made sure I was correct. There was a hotel on the far side of the street running perpendicular to mine, a dingy, rent-a-room-by-the-hour kind of place, whose entrance was just visible from where I parked. Laila had gone in twenty minutes earlier, and I was now waiting to see who she was going to meet. With Meredith's arrival, I had my answer.

As I watched intently, Meredith strolled in through the front door. Two minutes later, I received a text from the woman at the front desk, confirming that Meredith was heading upstairs to room 430. I had paid this woman a considerable amount of money to make certain Laila had a certain room that I had specially outfitted, and to notify me when she and whoever she was meeting arrived.

Despite myself, I smiled. This was a bigger prize than I had ever imagined when Lasinha asked me to begin surveillance of Laila. She was here in this universe investigating Ana's disappearance, which Lasinha claimed he knew nothing about. The implication being she had been taken by the Travelers. To prove he was not in any way involved, he allowed Laila to come to my universe and see what traces she could find of the missing Ana. And then he asked me to follow her, to see what I could discover.

He was hoping to discover the location of the hard drive containing the files with the reports on the Grand Regent, which Laila had hidden. Lasinha was convinced she had entrusted them to Ana, who had brought them to this universe, and that Laila would use the cover of the investigation to retrieve them. I did not uncover the files; instead I found, much to my disbelief, a nascent rebellion forming.

On its face, it seemed a dangerous risk, given the presence of the Order's compound, which Laila was certainly aware of. But her investigation into Ana's disappearance provided a useful cover for her to meet with Morris Loverne, coordinating her network where she thought there would be no ears to overhear what was being said. And now she was meeting with Meredith.

It was ingenious, in a way, I had to admit as my eyes followed a particularly attractive redhead in a yellow dress who was exiting the hotel. The traffic between the universes created by the Watchers' Order transferring Acolytes and apostates here and there would cover any signs of her own people's transfers to all but the most watchful eyes. Certainly I could only manage to track Laila's comings and goings, and that was only because of

Lasinha's assets on the other side.

To this point, he had simply tasked me with watching. I was not to act, and neither the rest of the Order nor the Grand Regent were to be informed of the matter. That would change now, with Meredith's arrival to the party. She was with the Grand Regent constantly, more than Lasinha himself. We could not allow her to continue to remain so near to him if she was truly plotting against the faith.

I gave Meredith five minutes to make her way to the hotel room and several more to allow Laila time to scan her for any surveillance devices before I activated my own in the room. The screen of my phone blinked to life and showed a black-and-white view of the room from on high. Meredith and Laila were sitting on the bed, near enough to touch each other, though they were both careful not to. They were speaking, but I couldn't hear them. I closed the view and went to the microphone app and played with the volumes until I could make out what they were saying and went back to the view of the room.

"You know what he's doing," Laila was saying. "Ana is—"

"Ana was a Society agent," Meredith said.

"No, we sent her there. I sent her. Because of Osahi."

"She was always with them," Meredith said, shaking her head. "You're a fool if you think otherwise. Her father was an agent from the beginning. You don't think he brought her in too?"

"No," Laila said, though she sounded doubtful.

It was pitiful to witness someone so deluded. I could only shake my head in amazement. How had I allowed myself to be so intimidated by her? Now she did not seem so difficult to read. She seemed desperate and sad.

Laila stood and turned so that she was facing the bed and Meredith, her back to me. On Meredith's face I could make out the need and the anger that I had seen that first day when I was inducted into the Order, which clearly fueled her. They stared at each other in a silence that was so icy that even I could feel it from where I sat in my car

"This is about all of us. All Regents," Laila said. "You're here because you know that to be true. You know that what the Acolytes and these Watchers are doing is wrong. Something must be done. That's why you're here."

Meredith gave a bitter laugh. "This isn't about all of us. It's about her and only her. You still love her."

I could see Laila flinch at the words, at the rawness in Meredith's voice. "Ana has been my friend since I joined the faith. I sent her away and I brought her back and I promised to protect her. And I have failed so miserably. But if you're asking if my feelings for her are like... The answer is no."

"Like *what*, Laila? Like your feelings for me? Oh, they were so deep and so true. You used me to get what you wanted, to make sure that you and Dejian and Lasinha could rule the faith. And then, as soon as it was convenient, you tossed me aside. Like I was nothing."

Meredith said the last with a fierceness that made me wince. Laila looked down at the floor, clenching and unclenching her hands.

"That's not true," she said. "That's not true. I cared very deeply about you, Meredith. I did. It hurt so much to send you away. But I had to. He made me. You know he made me. But I did it for the faith and because I thought you would understand."

"Oh, I understand, all too well. You can deny all you want, but I know what you are. You use people, Laila, you use and you use. Do you know he still calls your name out when we're together? He wanted me to dye my hair black. He wanted me..."

Meredith choked back the words and looked away from Laila for the first time. Her hands were kneading the covers on the bed, and I became fascinated by the unconsciousness of the gesture, so much so that I didn't notice at first that Laila had returned to the bed and was

27

sitting beside her.

"He wouldn't even touch me after he made me leave you," Laila said, shaking her head. "I was a fool. I was so wrong to send you away. It didn't make it better; it made it worse. It made him worse."

"He's a monster," Meredith said, swallowing back her tears.

They are talking about the Grand Regent. The thought took some time to fully settle in my mind. When it finally did, my hands began to shake so much that I had to set down the phone and listen without watching what was happening.

"He is," Laila said. "And we have to stop him before it's too late. Before he destroys the faith completely."

"And us," Meredith said.

I managed to control my emotions and pick up my phone to look again at the scene in the hotel room. Laila had put her arm around Meredith, who nestled her head against the other woman's shoulder. They both appeared to be crying. I felt like doing so myself. This was heresy. It was insurrection. It was apostasy and I was witnessing it.

"I'm sorry, Meredith," Laila said, after they both regained their composure. "I'm sorry for everything."

Meredith did not reply, but it appeared she tightened her embrace at the other woman's words.

"Will you help me to fight him?" Laila said, looking down into Meredith's eyes.

Meredith responded with kiss, tentative at first, but soon blossoming into much more. I watched until it was over, horror and desire warring within me. By the end I felt only fear tinged with excitement. There was a conspiracy at the very heart of the Church of Regents, and I would be the one to expose it.

5

I open my eyes and find myself in darkness. The soft hum of the register penetrates my consciousness, and for a moment I wonder where I am. Who I am. The gears of the elevator shift into motion down the hallway and I hear the door open. Someone enters or exits, then the door closes and the elevator lurches downward again. It brings me back to myself, back to this moment.

"David Aeida." I say the words to myself, luxuriating in the feeling of them. "David Aeida." That is who I am now. That is who I am.

I get to my feet and go to the window, pulling aside the blinds to look down on the campus. It is dark there, a twilit dark that promises to grow deeper. Snow is descending, collecting on the grass, though not yet upon the sidewalks and pathways. They are damp with puddles gathering in low spots.

I have no idea how long I have been here in my room. When last did I get up? Hours ago? Days? When did I eat? My complaining stomach tells me it has been some time. I glance around the shadowed quarters, but there is nothing immediately at hand. Briefly, I contemplate leaving and going to find food. The Grand Regent will have some in his quarters, or there will be a kitchen somewhere where they prepare it.

But I stay by the window, staring out at the snow, watching the individual flakes fall. Gradually my hunger dissipates, and I return to bed and lie with my eyes open, staring at the ceiling until once again I remember.

When I reported my findings to Lasinha, he was unsurprised, or at least gave every appearance of being so. He smiled and told me to keep up my surveillance of Laila.

"The most important thing is the files. We need to know where they are. Anything she says about that, report immediately to me."

I listened dumbfounded, unable to quite believe what I was hearing. "Aren't you worried about what they're planning? Shouldn't we inform the Grand Regent?"

"He will be informed. I will see to that. In the meantime, better to discover who is working with them and how deep this goes. They are not ready to attempt anything yet."

"I don't know that for certain."

Lasinha shook his head, still smiling. "If they were, we would know. They would have acted already. No, Laila will take her time. She will be careful. Which means we have time too."

He paused, lapsing into thought, before looking up at me. "It's Osahi who worries me. If they can bring him in, it will lead to trouble. Let me know immediately if you hear anything about him, or if you think they are moving. Otherwise, regular reports and continue as you were."

I did not share Lasinha's sense of complacence. The fate of the Church and the faith was being played out before my eyes, and he expected me to simply observe. He was not taking the matter as seriously as he should have. But he had not seen what I had seen or heard what I heard. The emotion, hurt, and conviction in the voices of Meredith and Laila were clear. They would not rest until they had destroyed the Grand Regent, and the faith with him.

But I had a greater part to play than that, I felt certain. If Lasinha did not see it, he would soon enough. I was going to take matters into my own hands.

I blink my eyes open again. A sound has disturbed my reverie. I wait a moment to see if it will return, whatever it was. All is quiet in the tower. Only the hum of the radiator disturbs the silence. I try to close my eyes, to return to my memories, but my thoughts will not let me. Questions keep intruding.

Why am I returning to old events? Old triumphs and failures? They were both, of course. Triumphs in the moment, only to transform into bitter failures as time went by. They led me here, to this place, where only memory remains as a solace. Yet I do not go where solace truly lies, but to those places where the ground was forever shifting and where I was left betrayed and broken by the faith I had given myself so utterly to.

I am now shaking with rage at what has befallen me, and rise to my feet and begin to pace the room to calm myself. But I cannot do so. The anger destroys any coherent thought I have. How could the Grand Regent do this to me, after all I have done for the faith? How could Lasinha abandon me and still abandon now? It is unfair. It is cruel.

A shriek pierces the night and quiets my rage. I am suddenly alert, poised and ready to act, though I have no sense of the source of the scream, or what I would do if I did know. But there is no doubt in my mind: this was the sound that stirred me from my reverie earlier. I wait to see if it will come again or if there is anything else to suggest where it came from.

As I wait, I go to the door, pressing my ear against it, to see if I can hear anyone in the hallway. A scrabbling sound, very faint, like an animal clawing against the inside of a wall, reaches my ears. Some sort of rodent, my instincts tell me, and I slip out the door into the hallway to investigate further.

Tiptoeing down the corridor—though I have no idea why I am taking such precautions—I pass the elevator and see the half-Morris standing sentinel outside the Grand Regent's rooms. Does he never sleep? He looks in my direction, his expression disinterested and blank. I nod and turn back. The sound is gone anyway.

It returns when I passed by Meredith's door. I stand outside, making sure that my shadow doesn't pass under and reveal my presence, and listen. The scrabbling is there, along with a low, keening moan, made ragged by sharp intakes of breath. It sounds utterly inhuman, but I know it is not.

I walk back to my room and return to my bed. Whatever rage and despair lies within me, it is nothing compared to Meredith.

One afternoon, after Laila met with Morris in a basement bar—a change from their usual arrangement, which made me wonder what it signified—I followed him instead of her when they went their separate ways. This was expressly against Lasinha's orders, but I decided it was not enough to simply keep following her, when Morris and Meredith and who knew who else from her network, were slipping into this universe and preparing their attack against the Grand Regent. I needed to know who was coming, and how they were doing so, in order to be able to disrupt them should the need arise.

As it inevitably would, for Lasinha would come to his senses soon enough. His obsession with the hard drive and files was blinding him to the peril Laila and her network posed. It was up to me to be prepared to disrupt her plans and her network, and I could not do so by simply following her.

It was difficult to glean much simply by observing

Laila. So long as she met her people in hotels, and made the arrangements with her phone, I could track her and make sure surveillance was in place. But she was far too clever for that, changing her meeting places and arrangements constantly so I could not anticipate anything.

Following her presented significant challenges. Not only was she good at shaking her tails, I could not stay close to her because she would recognize me. I had to track her phone, or, when she started turning it off, suspecting some sort of surveillance, the signature traces of her channel crossing. This was equipment Lasinha had gotten from his source in the Society, which they used to track people like us who had taken unauthorized crossings.

It was what I used to track Morris as well, for though he had never seen me in person, I took no risks and kept a healthy distance between us. He took me on a convoluted journey through several Vancouver neighborhoods, traveling by foot, bus, train, and cab. I remained in my car, never in sight of the vehicle he was in, so there was no possibility of his picking my tail. The Traveler device I mounted to the dash of my car. At a glance it would look like an overly large GPS, though any inspection of the screen would tell a different story.

This was less than ideal, of course, especially when Morris paused to linger anywhere. It left open the possibility of a hurried conversation or a package transfer with someone, anyone, all without my knowledge. My observation of Laila presented the same problems—I always knew where she was, but I wasn't always present when she was there. She had ample opportunity to retrieve the files from where Ana had hidden them, and pass them to someone else, who would then transfer them out of this universe, all without my knowing.

The abundance of caution Morris was practicing to ensure that he was not followed only confirmed my belief in my choice to follow him. Wherever he was going was important. It had to be the transfer point for Laila's network. If I had that, I had all I needed to end their little scheme.

At Alma and Broadway, he exited a bus and got into a car, reversing course back the way he had come, before turning onto West Fourth, where I had paused to determine where he was going. I cursed as he drove by, though he did not appear to look in my direction. After crisscrossing Broadway on various side streets for several blocks, to ensure that no one had picked up his trail, he started east, and I allowed myself to relax.

From there he left Vancouver. He obviously felt confident he had shaken any surveillance that might exist, for he proceeded on a direct route, with no doubling back or wandering. My worry at having potentially been made left as I became more and more mystified about where he was going. He went off the main highway and took a series of back roads into what passed for country in these parts. What, I wondered, could possibly be out here?

His vehicle came to a stop outside a farmhouse at the end of a road. By the time I realized that the road terminated, it was too late—I was already in sight of the house and anyone who might be watching. I pulled off to the side of the road and sat sweating and wondering if Morris would remember my car from earlier. There was little I could see of the house. The yard it was in was surrounded by trees, revealing only the top floor and several windows that would provide good observation points of the road and anyone approaching.

This whole thing threatened to turn into a disaster, blowing up my surveillance of Laila and sending her whole network underground before I had a chance to discover anything. But she was not here, I told myself, and Morris did not know me—and, if I was lucky, hadn't noticed me earlier. Even if he had, he likely only remembered the car. There were a lot of silver Toyota Corollas on the road. That was why I had chosen it.

I got out of the car and decided to put on a show,

popping the hood and feigning studying the engine with a worried look on my face. After poking around for a bit and shaking my head, I closed the hood and pulled out my cell phone. More head shaking followed, and I put it away and got back in my car. When I did, I saw that Morris' signature trace had vanished. He had crossed over. And I had found Laila's transfer point.

I studied the device's screen to make certain Morris was gone, but there could be no doubt. The steady pulse I had followed along the map all the way out to this isolated house had disappeared. That did not mean the house was empty or that I was unwatched. It would be wise to recruit someone from this world to keep an eye on the transfer equipment. That had been my first role in the Church with Lasinha and Ana.

The smart, cautious move would have been to leave and not risk discovery. Put the house under observation and see what could be learned. I was not in a position to do that, and neither was I so inclined. A decision made, I took the screen down from the dash, hid it in the glove box, and started the car. I drove slowly down the rest of the road, following the path that wound around the yard and up behind the house to where Morris' car was parked.

I turned off the car and waited, thrumming my fingers on the wheel. No one emerged from inside the house. Nodding to myself, I got out and looked around. The house was set on a small rise, surrounded by a bright green lawn that stretched out to the surrounding row of trees. The grass had been freshly cut, perhaps that morning. In the distance I could hear a car approaching from a nearby road, leading to a moment of panic, which quickly dissipated along with the sound of the car as it turned in another direction.

"Okay," I said, in an affirmation to myself. No more delaying.

I went up to the door and knocked several times, receiving no response. When enough time had passed, I tried the door and found it locked. After a quick and pointless glance around—there was clearly nobody around for miles—I picked the lock and slipped inside, finding myself in an empty house.

The interior was as innocuous and uninteresting as its exterior. There were few signs that anyone lived here regularly. It had the smell and look of a safe house, anonymous and little used. The cupboards were filled with cans of food and noodle packages, while the fridge was empty and unplugged. By all appearances, no one stayed for long.

I combed through the rooms until I found what I was looking for in a linen closet upstairs. Transfer equipment, still warm from Morris' journey. It was of a recent vintage, though not so new as the Order's equipment. How had Laila acquired it? With Ana gone, she no longer had a source in the Society, though perhaps that was not the case. Perhaps there was more we didn't know.

It was a simple matter for me to get the various dates, times, and coordinates of every transfer that had taken place using the box. I spent half an hour jotting down the most recent transfers with a scrap of paper I retrieved from the car. Later I would check these against my surveillance of Laila and see how many crossings there had been in addition to the meetings with Morris and Meredith. By a simple count, I guessed there were at least twice as many, and once I had translated the coordinates, I would have a better idea of who else might have been coming over and from where.

Before I left, I did another sweep of the house to see if there was anything else to uncover. I found nothing, and the car, similarly, revealed nothing of interest. By then I had been there for almost an hour, and I thought I would be pressing my luck to stay any longer, even though the transfer box's records showed no crossings occurring on the same day. Best not to chance it. And best not to risk revealing my presence by putting a tracer on the car or any other surveillance equipment in the house, as tempting as that was. If they were smart, they swept after every crossing.

I drove back to Vancouver, feeling satisfied with myself and in control of the situation. Lasinha would be pleased when he found out what I had been up to, I felt certain. My disobeying of orders had put us in a position to destroy Laila's uprising. The day was glorious, the sun high in a vibrant blue sky empty of clouds, and I decided to take a detour to small bar I knew near Main and Broadway. It had a patio where I could enjoy the sun and a pint of beer and let my thoughts wander where they would.

6

There is a knock upon my door that startles me awake. Was I asleep, or simply remembering? The distinction is hard for me to make these days.

I feel awful, haggard and drawn, my throat dry and my stomach pinched in agony. The remains of a meal, a plate and some crumbs, sit on the night table beside the bed, but I have no sense of how long ago that was. It may have been days; it may have been last night. Who is to say?

The knocking continues, ebbing and flowing in volume, and I have the distinct impression that it was going on for some time before I woke. I stumble to the door and pull it open, blinking as light floods in, penetrating the darkness of my solitary quarters. Meredith stands on the other side, glaring into the shadows and at me.

"You look awful," she says. "Clean yourself up. The Grand Regent wants to see you."

I nod and step back to allow her to enter. Her lip curls in distaste. "I'll wait out here, thank you. How long has it been since you showered?"

I flush, her insult jarring me from my stupor. There is a retort on my lips about what I overheard the other night—

her own particular battle with the long darkness—but I resist the urge. That knowledge may be useful later; best to keep it in reserve now. Instead I close the door in her face and go to the bathroom and take a shower.

She is still standing outside my door when I emerge twenty minutes later, the same glare upon her face.

"I need something to eat," I say, as I risk a glance down the corridor at the alcove and the window out of the tower. It is light out, but other than that, I can glean little about the time of day, and my body offers no answers. It remains sluggish and dull.

Meredith shrugs. *Not my problem*, her expression says. She leads me down the corridor past the half-Morris and into the audience room. The Grand Regent sits upon his throne, a finger upon his pursed lips. He is frowning, but his expression suggests perplexity rather than anger. That can surface at any moment, as I am only too aware.

"I've brought him," Meredith says without preamble or niceties. Hers are the harsh words of someone who no longer cares what the Grand Regent does to her.

He appears not to notice, turning to look at me, a slightly confused expression on his face. "Ah, Aeida," he says. "My faithful vessel. We have much to discuss."

"Grand Regent," I say, bowing slightly.

He waves at me to approach the throne, which I do. Meredith has already left, disappearing back into the corridor, not even bothering to ask him for leave to do so. It is a shocking insult, yet the Grand Regent appears unconcerned. If he is aware that she has come and gone, he does not show it.

"The faith has been betrayed, David Aeida," he says, shaking his head sadly. "We are beset on all sides by our enemies."

"That is why we have the Order, Grand Regent," I say.

"The Watchers. Lasinha and the Acolytes convinced me of their necessity. Now I wonder how wise I was to put my trust in them."

"They will not betray you."

"You did, and you were one of them."

I wince. "That is true. My betrayal was a personal one, though, Grand Regent. Not a matter of the faith. I would never betray the faith."

"The faith and personal are intermingled, David Aeida. They are inseparable, as we both know intimately." He smiles, a wistful smile, as though remembering something.

I let out my breath, only realizing as I do so how my chest is aching from holding it.

"No, Aeida, there is much to be done. Much to be done," the Grand Regent says. "The Society sends its agents against me, again and again. They are unrelenting. They have subverted those closest to me, sometimes without their even realizing it. That is why I need you to search Laila's mind. To find out how deep the worm has rooted. She will help me. In her heart, she was a faithful vessel. She only did what she thought necessary."

"I am searching," I say. "But I have found little so far. She guards her thoughts closely."

"She would," he says. "She would. Keep trying. The times are faulty. The times are faulty. Our vesseldom makes us weak. Frail. I only want to restore the strength that was stolen from us by the Society and their ilk. How many worlds have they infected? They go from universe to universe, tearing its fabric asunder, and yet they would deny us our true, whole selves. How many lives have they destroyed without explanation? How many universes have they made their own, where no whisper of them was even known?"

I nod. These are questions every Regent asks of themselves. Where did the Travelers come from? Why did they come to this universe and not my own? Surely they have their reasons, but none are clear to me. Perhaps it is simply arbitrary, for all their talk of ensuring the universes remain uncorrupted, which makes their work against the Church of Regents all the more sinister.

The Grand Regent is similarly lost in thought, again touching a finger to his pursed lips as he stares across the room at an image of the Mayan calendar. "The fate of ourselves and our universes is at stake, Aeida," he says. "Make no mistake. This is an eternal struggle—the ultimate struggle. We must not lose. We must do everything we can. Everything."

"Yes, Grand Regent," I say. "May I ask you something?"

He glances at me with a look of faint surprise, as though he has only just registered my presence beside him on the dais. I shift my feet uncomfortably, and he nods. "Of course, Aeida. You are a faithful vessel."

"Thank you," I say, casting my eyes down. "It is about the Watchers' Order. I know it is the ultimate bulwark against the Travelers and the heresy of the faithful. But I have not seen any of its members here. Or the Acolytes, for that matter."

The Grand Regent gives me a sage smile. "Always the observer, Aeida. The Order is still here." He waves his hand around as though to encompass the whole campus. "The Acolytes have decamped for safer climes. The Travelers are watching us closely, especially here. We cannot afford to risk their work. They have hidden themselves. But rest assured—I still have means of contacting them."

"Of course," I say. "A prudent course. Why have you not hidden yourself, if I may ask?"

"I must be visible to the faithful. I am the center of the faith. I am De Gofroy's heir. He has granted me his wisdom and graced me with a connection to his true soul and his other selves. He is guiding me to the one universe. I must guide the rest of the Regents, and to do so I must be here, at the center of the faith."

"I understand," I say, and then hesitate. I have left the question I most want answered to the end. "And what of Lasinha? Does he still—"

I am unable to finish. The Grand Regent stands up, fire in his eyes, leveling a finger at my face.

"Never utter that name in my presence."

I open my mouth and close it, unable to find the words, my mind refusing to work. What has befallen Lasinha? Tendrils of fear worm their way through my stomach. Have I damaged the little trust I have built with the Grand Regent?

"You may go," the Grand Regent says with a wave as he returns to his throne. He does not glance in my direction as I leave.

Despite my worries that I have irrevocably damaged my relationship with the Grand Regent, Meredith returns the next day to summon me again into his presence. He makes no mention of our discussion yesterday, beckoning me to join him upon the dais. Morris stays in the audience room this time, vigilantly watching us, his expression a blank mask.

"Aeida, my faithful vessel. It is good to have you near in these faulty times. The Travelers have subverted all those closest to me, without their realizing it. It is incredible. That is why I need you. And Laila. Together we can find out how deep the poison has sunk. She will help me. And you will too. You were both always faithful vessels at heart."

I swallow at these words. He appears to have forgotten yesterday entirely, for these are so like the words he spoke then.

"Of course," I say. "I am trying. "But I have found little so far. She guards her thoughts closely."

"She would," he says. "She would. You must keep trying."

"I will," I say, and offer nothing else. This time I understand that my role is simply to be present and to hear what the Grand Regent has to say. My own opinions and questions are of no consequence, and to give voice to my thoughts would be a hindrance in his eyes.

"I have been thinking lately of my other selves," the Grand Regent says. "The other Lasinhas, the other Lailas. The other Aeidas. He is not a Regent, the one in this universe. He lives in Vancouver, near Marine Drive. An ugly little place. I had the Order follow him for a time. He passed by our Protocol Center nearly every day and never once went in. Yet you committed yourself absolutely to the faith. Strange isn't it?"

It is not something I have wondered about too deeply, my self in this universe. I've known for some time that he is not a Regent and, as such, he does not interest me particularly. His is a path I did not take in some senses, though mine was never available to him. Like all the rest of the Aeidas, he is not me, even if we are all part of a truer Aeida. Our experiences have made us other to ourselves, and that is part of the tragedy of the universes, and part of the utter cruelty of the Society. That is my sense of things, anyway.

I say none of this and let the Grand Regent continue to expound.

"It is an odd thing. I have, of course, limited my journeys to the other universes—the Travelers watch me far too closely—and I have never had the opportunity to investigate myself. Lasinha, Laila, and I made it an unspoken rule to avoid our other selves and most of the other selves of the Hierarchy. Apparently it is something the Society watches for in their study of the universes. People are drawn to their other selves—it's simple curiosity, of course—and interacting with them would raise many alarms.

"But it does make one wonder. Am I, as I am, more or less in the other universes? Are you? Would the Laila of another universe have been more loyal to me, or less? If you could replace me with another me, would that person lead the faith as I do? Make the same choices I have made? Would De Gofroy bestow his blessing upon me? Would his true self provide me with his visions, his guidance to the true universe?"

I do not know how to answer any of these questions, but the Grand Regent is not interested in my answers. He is talking to himself and I am merely here as decoration. This interest in his other self, in all our other selves, worries me, though. Neither De Gofroy nor Molijc, after he succeeded to the Grand Regency, spoke much of our doubles in the other universes. They spoke of uniting all our Regent selves with our true beings, but there was no sense that we needed to enlist the others in the cause in any way. The other selves would follow so long as we provided a path for them to do so.

My concern only grows as the Grand Regent turns to me. "You have grown very quiet, David Aeida."

"Yes, Grand Regent," I say. "Your words concern me, I must admit."

"Why, Aeida?" He seems curious, which worries me even more, his gaze intent upon me.

"As you say yourself, Grand Regent, we cannot risk contacting our other selves. The Society watches us closely enough as it is. That would be the sort of thing that would give them the justification to end the faith."

He waves a dismissive hand at me. "The Travelers will never know what I do. They are always a step or two behind. How many times have I crossed over? How many times have we all? Under their very noses. The Order operates with impunity in the universes and will continue to do so. We commit enough crimes in their eyes to end the faith should they choose. They dare not, because they know our power."

I frown, but say nothing. A moment ago he was railing against the Travelers and their agents as corrupters of the faith, the seeds of our destruction, and now he is dismissing their power to stop him entirely.

"No, Aeida, this warrants further investigation. That is why when Osahi came to me with his plan, I approved it.

Most ingenious, Osahi. Though not to be trusted, of course."

Osahi. *What has he done?* I recall the strange house in his compound and the man with the oddly familiar voice. That is the man Osahi is going to bring to the Grand Regent. But what is his plan? Whatever it is, it is not what the Grand Regent thinks.

I open my mouth to say so, but the Grand Regent waves his hand.

"That is enough, Aeida. We will talk more soon enough. All will become clear to you in time. You must find the answers I am looking for in Laila. I have matters of the faith to attend to now. And Regents to offer my blessings to."

He stands up from his throne and motions to Morris Loverne, whose presence I had forgotten. Morris gives a stiff nod and turns to open the door. I move off the dais toward the door and stand by as several Regents march in. They are moving in single file, their expressions as blank as Loverne's. Despite my best efforts, I am unable to resist a shudder.

Or to leave, even though the Grand Regent has bid me to go. He does not seem to notice me, and I watch with fascination as these half-things assemble before him. From my vantage point beside Loverne, I can see them all, and I realize that their faces are all familiar. The High Regents are there, those that remain loyal to the Church, and others who I know but cannot place.

It comes to me with a sudden shock of realization. These are the faithful who gathered that first day when the Grand Regent introduced me. My skin goes cold and clammy, and I feel as though I might faint or vomit. They are all creatures of the Acolytes.

Morris places a hand upon me as those gathered all kneel upon the floor to pray. He looks at me with his empty eyes and then at the door. I nod, not needing to be told twice, and hurry out. Behind me, I can hear the Grand

45

Regent begin to speak.

"Welcome, all. Welcome. Let us pray."

7

For a week, my routine with the Grand Regent continues. He summons Meredith, who summons me, and I sit with him on the dais while he confides whatever is upon his mind. Mostly he rages about the Society and those in the faith who have betrayed him. Lasinha remains unmentioned, though obviously at the forefront of his mind. Laila he talks of frequently, exhorting me to discover her secrets.

Someday he will demand I reveal what I have found, and I will have to lie or admit I cannot find her in my mind. That she is gone. I do not know what will happen to me then. Will he summon the Acolytes to try to find her?

These thoughts haunt my every discussion with him. I know my time is short, but I don't know how long I have. And I must convince him to remove Laila from my mind. If I can do that, whatever happens after will not matter. I will at least be in possession of this body and mind and can do as I wish without any other concern.

All this leaves aside Osahi and whatever he is planning. I am certain it is the overthrow of the Grand Regent, as that is what Osahi has always desired since Molijc's rise to power. Given how paranoid and isolated the Grand

Regent currently is, having sent Lasinha and all his other advisers away, he no doubt sees this as his chance. I fear he is correct. But it is also my chance, and I must ensure that I make good on it before Osahi does.

I see little of Meredith, beyond when she comes to summon me, and hear little more when we are in our respective quarters, though I listen intently for a repeat of her succumbing to despair. The quiet of the tower, with no one coming to visit the Grand Regent, except his menagerie of half-things, begins to seem ominous, and my memories beckon as they once did.

To ease my mind, and to give me something to keep me preoccupied while I await my next summons, I start to explore the campus and the tower. I need to know if things are as perilous as I fear they are. Again I find empty buildings and empty pathways wherever I go. There seems to be no one in any of the Hierarchy buildings, which once hummed with activity, if Laila's memories are to be trusted.

Even the Acolyte building on the north side of campus, where few dared to enter, has an abandoned feel. The walls are filled with scratches and holes where equipment was unbolted, and the floors are marked by the outlines of vast apparatuses that once occupied those spaces. Now there are only bits and pieces of detritus remaining—screws and bolts and other pieces not considered valuable enough to bring along. To where?

I think back to the compound Lasinha and I established in my universe. There will be others like it, and that is where the Acolytes will be. Given the upheavals in the Hierarchy, the infiltrations by the Travelers, it seems a sensible precaution. Yet this cannot help but feel like the signs of a retreating army, taking all that it can carry with it. Which makes me the thief and grave robber come to steal gold teeth from the corpses and take away whatever other scraps remain.

None of this explains where the faithful are. The

Hierarchy, the Initiates, and other Regents, who flocked to the campus to practice their Protocols at the feet of De Gofroy and Molijc. They all populated this place and made it run. Even the cleaning and maintenance staff—Regents all, presumably—are nowhere to be found, and the evidence of their absence is obvious. Dust and refuse litter many of the rooms, garbage receptacles are overflowing, and the temperature in the buildings fluctuates wildly. It all speaks to a place abandoned.

Yet we were met by Watchers as soon as we crossed over to this world, and had to fight our way through to reach the Grand Regent. They were expecting us, of course, and had prepared our welcome. Osahi and Suon saw to that. My memories of that are disjointed, given the internal struggle that was underway between myself and Laila, but the corridors we walked down did not feel as empty, as absent as this.

It is only when I go to the physical plant where we crossed over, which is on the edge of the church campus grounds, that I receive my answer. The Order is there standing guard, armed and not even bothering to hide it. At my approach, two turn to face me, leveling their pulse rifles on me.

"Return to the tower," one says, in a booming voice. Under his breath, he says to the woman standing beside him, "Another one on the fritz?"

"I'm not one of them," I say, holding up my hands, though I realize that is not precisely true. No one feels the weight of the Acolytes' hands upon them more than me.

Still, I turn and retreat the way I came. After my confrontation, I make a circuit around the campus, and my suspicions are confirmed. The Watchers stand vigil around the entire grounds, armed and ready to attack should anyone attempt to enter. Or leave.

I watched Laila and her compatriots for weeks, reporting my findings to Lasinha, who always told me to continue my observation.

"We have enough to move against them now," I said. "We know the major players. I would guess we have half her network right now. The more time we give them, the more time they will have to put contingencies in place."

"It's a risk," Lasinha admitted. "But one I'm willing to take if it means we get the entire network."

I doubted that was possible, for the longer we waited, the more chances we gave Laila to expand and hide that network, but I held my tongue. A new idea had lately taken hold in my mind, and, as I continued my observation of Laila and the farmhouse, the temptation was slowly growing for me to act upon it. I had yet to tell Lasinha about the house east of the city, saving that revelation for when he unleashed the shackles he had put on me.

But just because I couldn't use the house and its transfer equipment to destroy Laila's network, didn't mean I couldn't use it for my own ends. The more I thought about it, the more compelling the idea became. Lasinha would be furious, of course, but he was actively subverting an investigation of the Watchers' Order for his own purposes, whatever they might be. If he called me out on my own mercenary actions, I intended to reply in kind, for his were much more likely to threaten the faith.

I went back and forth on the matter, even as I carefully took steps to put in place my plan, so that I would be ready to act when I had decided. My reasoning was that if I decided against it, I could easily abandon what I had started, but that was not the way of things. Once I had begun surreptitiously collecting all the crossing traffic at the compound and analyzing it, my decision had effectively been made. There was no reasonable explanation for my doing so, and once I got away with it, there was no particular reason for me to stop. My plan went forward, carried by the internal combustion of its own logic, even as I agonized over every step.

That it was wrong, I knew. But then, so much of what

we did with the Order was morally questionable, even if it was in defense of the faith. I had dealt with the shame and the doubts, the questions I could not answer without feeling ill. Those were all gone now. It was necessary for the protection of the faith. And, if necessary, I could justify this as well.

The first time was the most rewarding. Routine sets in so quickly, and even this was no different. But that initial attempt was so filled with fear at the idea of being caught, and what would happen to me, that when it actually worked as I intended, the success was all the sweeter. Later, I would become complacent, certain that I had fooled those who watched me, arrogant in my certainty.

Though there was little in the way of a pattern to the crossings at the farmhouse, I had managed to determine that it was most likely to be empty in the hours after midnight. From four in the morning on, transfers would begin to allow those who arrived time to reach their appointment with Laila or others. That meant I could bring someone across without too much concern, provided I deleted the crossing details from the transfer equipment. It would not hide the crossing from someone who knew how to look, but so long as Laila's people didn't realize their house was compromised, I saw little reason to worry.

That was the simplest part of my plan. I knew when to open the channels and where to. I knew how to cover my tracks so that Laila's people and the other Watchers would not discover what I was doing. What was more difficult was letting the person on the other side know when to come without anyone else being the wiser. I could not cross over myself, although that would have been the simplest. Given the equipment the Order had in our compound, my having done so would be obvious and my whole scheme would quickly be found out.

Instead I cultivated my trust within the Watchers, and particularly within the compound, to get what I wanted.

There were still routine transfers of material, like those Lasinha initially had me supervise before the Order's creation. They were now handled by various Regents Lasinha had inducted into the lower levels of the Order, while the transfers of people were overseen by people like me. The apostate crossings, as I called them, resulted in heightened security and clearing of the lower levels of the compound of all but authorized personnel.

The routine crossings occurred on a regular schedule, with no one paying any particular mind to them. Which meant there was an opportunity, and I seized it. I chose a time when I knew Lasinha would not be in this universe. He had a nose for this sort of subterfuge, and I wanted him absent. I also selected the most credulous of the Regents overseeing the transfers, in my judgment, appearing in the transfer room just as he initiated the crossings.

"This was supposed to go too," I said, waving a small box imperiously before I set it upon the crate.

The Regent, whose name I did not even know, frowned, uncertain of how to handle this departure from protocol. The box had all the markings of a Watcher courier parcel, and if he chose to inspect it closely, he would see it numbered and categorized as such messages normally were. If he looked it up in the system, he would find it matched one sent several days before, on a different transfer to a different Order site. A clerical error, I would claim, should the question come. He would never dare open the box—I was his superior and it was an official Order courier, which could only be opened by its intended recipients, or someone in Lasinha's position.

I did not stop once I put the parcel on the crate, calling out thanks and heading out of the transfer room without so much as a glance in the Regent's direction. It was all routine, not worth questioning or thinking about, my whole attitude said. I paused outside the transfer room to listen, ostensibly replying to a text or an email on my phone, and waited until I heard the transfer go through.

The day that followed passed in an agony of suspense, only somewhat relieved when I arrived at the farmhouse at one in the morning. No questions had been raised, or at least none had been returned to the compound, by my parcel, which was promising. But it still remained to be seen if the crossing would go ahead, if the courier request would be obeyed.

If it was not, if there were doubts about its authenticity, and an investigation was conducted, I was prepared. The farmhouse was the transfer hub of Laila's network; the only plausible reason for a crossing to here was if someone from that network was involved. If there were questions about what I was doing in the house, I would reveal I had been aware of it for some time. There would be more questions and doubts, but I would have answers for them all. I had witnessed Order interrogations, I knew the questions they would ask, and it was easy to come up with answers while I was far away from any Watcher cell.

It was far too easy to tell myself my lies would be convincing, but the only one who believed was me.

The house was empty when I arrived, as I had expected, and I sat down to wait, glancing at my phone every minute or so to confirm that the crossing time hadn't passed. As it grew nearer and nearer, various doom-laden scenarios flashed through my mind, the best of which was that no crossing occurred and I was left to wonder about who knew and what. The worst was that the crossing did take place, but some Black Robes came through the channel, disappearing me forever.

None of these possibilities was at all comforting, and I found I could no longer simply sit and wait for the inevitable. A dozen times I told myself I should leave before it was too late. Before I crossed over this latest line, another in a long line from which I knew there would be no turning back.

Instead I went upstairs and paced from room to room,

wiping sweat from my brow. That was where I was when the channels opened. The air changed first before the channel was visible, and I shuddered despite myself, overcome by guilt and shame. What was I doing? Yet I remained.

As I had hoped, the channel opened downstairs, in the living room. I stayed upstairs, keeping an eye on the transfer equipment, ready to close the channel if something looked amiss. Nothing did, and when the sensation of the other universe finally vanished, I made my way tentatively downstairs and peered into the living room.

My trepidation was for nothing, though. There, awaiting me alone, was Ana, looking as gloriously beautiful as I remembered. I felt my face go red, a flurry of emotions swarming me as I stared at her, before taking a tentative step into the room. She looked up at my approach, a blank, unrecognizing stare on her face.

"Hello, Ana," I said with a smile.

It is the middle of the night, and I am lost in a tangle of memory, dream, remorse, and self-pity, when there is a knock at the door. As always, Meredith is on the other side, with the same possessed and prying look on her face. Her hair and makeup are as precise as always, despite the late hour, which leaves me even more unsettled than I already am in my disheveled state.

"The Grand Regent wishes to see you," she says, the barest hint of a smile on her face. "Now," she adds, letting me know that I do not have the luxury of preparing myself.

I quickly pull on whatever clothes lie at hand and splash a little water on my face to try to wake myself. Meredith leads the way to the audience chamber as I struggle to lift my mind from its haze before we arrive. It is odd that I am being summoned at such an hour, which suggests this is not to be one of my regular conversations with the Grand Regent. That suspicion is confirmed as we enter the chamber and I see Osahi, De Vroes, and Suon all gathered there. Meredith, as opposed to her normal practice when summoning me, remains standing beside me. We all look to the Grand Regent.

He smiles. "Thank you for coming before me. I know the hour is late, but the occasion is momentous. For some time now, I have been struggling with maintaining my connection with the true self of the great De Gofroy. The visions he sent me have become infrequent, the connection of my self to his haphazard. I suspect it is because his soul has journeyed farther from this universe in the last years and soon it will become impossible for me to reach him at all."

The Grand Regent pauses to look from face to face, as though to see whether we understand the gravity of the situation. He continues. "It is essential for the faith that I maintain this tenuous link with De Gofroy for as long as possible. He knows the way to the true universe. He can guide us. And Regents everywhere know his genius in these matters. We all do.

"Now, thanks to Osahi's efforts, we have a means of extending my connection with De Gofroy, deepening it. With his guidance restored, we shall overcome the Travelers' poisonous influence upon the faith. We shall overthrow the apostates who would have all Regents remain partial beings, disunited."

He says the last in a ringing voice that echoes across the audience room. I feel none of his triumph, for I understand now what Osahi has done. The voice, familiar and yet foreign, of the man in house was De Gofroy. Another De Gofroy, from that universe or some other. Someone who will tell the Grand Regent what he wants to hear and guide him to his doom. He will ensure that Osahi is triumphant and that I will be left to battle Laila in this flesh for all the time that remains to it.

As I look on helplessly, trying and failing to find some way to stop what is happening, the Grand Regent beckons

Osahi to the dais and draws him into an embrace. He is weeping, I see, overcome by the moment, while Osahi's expression remains as impenetrable as always. I glance at Meredith and see that she is looking at me, both of us wondering how the other is handling this terrible moment. An ironic, bitter smile crosses her lips and vanishes before she turns back to the dais.

"Thank you, Grand Regent," Osahi says in a haughty voice. "It was with much hard work and great sacrifice by my people, faithful Regents all, that we managed to bring the other De Gofroy here to save the faith. We battled the Society; we thwarted the Seekers. And now he is here to give voice to De Gofroy."

He waves and Suon goes to the door and opens it. Two women I do not recognize enter, and in between them is a man I do. He is both familiar and yet unfamiliar in the same instance. For one, I never met De Gofroy; I have only Laila's memories to guide me. The man before us is heavier than De Gofroy ever was, his face gone jowly and his hair much sparser and whiter. He slouches and walks with a slightly halting gait, having none of the vitality and presence the De Gofroy of this universe possessed. But then, this man is older than De Gofroy ever was.

And there can be no doubting it is De Gofroy. *A* De Gofroy, at least. There is a glint to his eyes and a knowing smirk that I recognize as his own.

The Grand Regent is speechless at the sight of his former master, a look of awe upon his face. "I cannot tell you how I have longed for this moment, Grand Regent."

A broad smile seizes De Gofroy's face. "I am not the Grand Regent. You are. I am not even a Regent. All this talk is new to me. I am simply a former lieutenant. A doctor. A philosopher. A dabbler in all manner of science."

His voice is arresting, and very different from the De Gofroy of this universe. It is not just his accent, which is shifted somewhat from the vaguely mid-Atlantic tones of this universe's De Gofroy, and which is not of any place in this world and my own. His voice is cracked and worn, deepened and scarred by cigarettes and alcohol, his bulbous nose suggesting he more than enjoys his drink.

"Yes," the Grand Regent says, momentarily taken aback. "Yes. Of course. That makes sense...of course. The Church has not come to your universe. Or the Society."

De Gofroy shakes his head. "The first I heard of any of this was when my dear friend Toma came to me and told me of the desperate battle you are all engaged in. As a man of science, I find it fascinating. Multiple universes. I have theorized on the matter considerably. And to be proven right and yet so wrong, all in the same moment, is incredible. Wonderful."

"Yes, I imagine so," the Grand Regent says, in a warm voice.

He is, I can tell, overcome by emotion and still not entirely convinced that this is not his own De Gofroy resurrected somehow. Osahi knew this would happen. He knew how paranoid and suggestible the Grand Regent is at this juncture and how he might use that to his own advantage.

"I would be delighted to speak with you on such matters and others," the Grand Regent says.

"I would be delighted as well," De Gofroy says. "I'm sure we will have much to discuss."

"Yes. We stand upon the cusp of greatness, I feel. Much depends on the days that lie ahead. Come. I would like to speak to you on these matters."

The Grand Regent waves at De Gofroy to follow him and steps off the dais, heading toward the rooms behind the audience chamber. De Gofroy, after a moment's hesitation and a glance at Osahi, who nods, follows behind. The rest of us remain where we are, watching as the two men go and the door is closed behind them.

As soon as it is closed, Osahi steps off the dais and goes to consult with Suon, De Vroes, and the two women who brought the other De Gofroy with them. I watch them whisper to each other, alternating between fury and despondency, my body shaking with the roiling emotion. All I am able to overhear is Osahi's final edict to De Gofroy's keepers.

"He is not to leave here without your being with him. As soon as one of them emerges, send word to me."

He, Suon, and De Vroes go to leave, all of them glancing over to where Meredith and I stand. Neither of us has moved since the Grand Regent and De Gofroy left, both of us still a little stunned at what has taken place. Osahi continues toward the door, the other two trailing behind him.

"You think this ends things?" Meredith says as the half-Morris stiffly opens the door. "You couldn't be more wrong."

"I think the faith will soon be in safer hands and this madness will be at an end," Osahi says, turning back to glare at her. "I don't need to remind you of your part in this. Or your other failures."

Meredith smiles. "You can't resist, can you? And no matter what happens with Molijc, you won't be able to resist when the Acolytes come. Make no mistake, they will have their say on this. You, Laila, me, Lasinha, we can all be cast aside. But not them."

"We shall see about that," Osahi says, defiant and confident.

"Ask him how that will go," Meredith says, pointing at De Vroes.

"We shall see," Osahi says again, as though all this has already been decided and it is a matter of time.

I can see De Vroes' face darken with emotion, his expression troubled. His eyes flick from Meredith's to my own. Osahi and Suon have already moved out the door toward the elevator. The renegade Acolyte moves to follow them, but not before he casts another lingering glance in our direction.

TWO:

A FAITH CONFIRMED

8

Morris Loverne sat across from me, his face drawn and haggard, his eyes sunk into his face and red around their edges. When had he last slept? When had I, for that matter? It felt as though we had been running for days and days, chased by some nightmare we could not escape. The faith had become a nightmare, my life one of unending horror as I realized what was being done in its name. And I was powerless to stop it all.

"You weren't followed?"

Morris grimaced. "I don't even know anymore."

"Me either. One can hope, I suppose."

"That is in short supply, I'm afraid," Morris said.

We smiled at one another. What else could we do?

I got up from my chair and went to peer out from behind the curtains of the apartment window, which had been drawn tight before I entered, as per my instructions. Below I could see the river and the pathway that snaked alongside it, overgrown by grass and trees in some places. In the distance I could see the towers of the Church rising above the rest of the city.

It was dangerous to be meeting here in our own universe, so near to Molijc and the Acolytes and the

Watchers' Order, but I felt I had no choice. We had only recently learned that the Watchers had the equipment necessary to track us when we crossed into other universes. Lasinha had somehow stolen it from the Travelers. Which meant that all our work and careful planning had been for naught. Our network was exposed, and it was only a matter of time before Lasinha gave the order to move against us. Why he hadn't already was something of a mystery.

We were here now to try to see what, if anything, could be salvaged from this mess. Yet I could not shake my unease that I was still being watched, that this too would fail. The scans of the rooms had revealed no listening devices or cameras, and I had lost my tails early on in the morning. Morris and I had selected this place months ago and had not set foot in it. Nor had anyone from our network. It was here for this eventuality, long dreaded, now here.

"There's nothing to be seen from up here," Morris said from where he sat on the couch. "No sense worrying about it. If they've found this place, then they've found everything and we're done."

"We're done," I said, letting the curtain go and heading over to the kitchen. "The only thing I can't figure out is why we're still here. Why hasn't the Order taken us?"

I opened various cupboards until I find an unsealed bottle of bourbon and a couple of glasses. Taking them over to the living room, I poured both Morris and myself a measure, and sat across from him in a deep chair that felt as though it might absorb me. I raised my glass, and he did the same.

"So," he said, and took a sip.

"So," I said. Another smile passed between us. "They're waiting for something. This is our opportunity."

"They have to be ready to scoop up over half the network. No one will be in a position to do anything if we try something."

I nodded. "There will be a small window before they realize what we're doing and can stop us. Meredith will be the key. She can get us close to Molijc before the Watchers can act."

"Do you trust her?" Morris said, his expression indicating that he did not.

"No," I said, then shook my head and took another sip of whiskey. "It would be foolish of me to. All the same, we have to try. This may be our only chance. We try and see if she is as good as her word."

"Right," Morris said. He did not agree, but he offered no argument. "And if she isn't?"

I mulled this for a time. "Let's give her the chance to prove herself trustworthy. I'll offer myself up. And we'll see what she does. Tell everyone to be ready to for the uprising. But they should also have their exits ready, just in case Meredith screws us. You especially. You'll need to lead this if things go badly."

Morris frowned. He clearly expected things to go badly. "What about you?"

"That's the other thing we have to do," I said. "We have to find a way out of this for me. If the Acolytes put their tamp on me or scrape me or whatever else they do, I need to be able to come back. There has to be a way. We know the things they create are unstable. Do you think you can find that out?"

Morris considered that for a moment, staring at the whiskey in his glass. "I think so. I'll talk to my Acolyte source. I think he'll help us."

"Good," I said, and downed the rest of my drink. "Let's get to it."

I come to, gasping for air and fighting with the bed covers. My skin is slick with sweat and I am shivering so much from the cold that for a moment I wonder if I am suffering from a fever. It is not, though I almost wish it were. That would be easier.

The memory I have just emerged from was Laila's, not mine. Its details are already vanishing, like a dream after waking, but I am quite certain it was not one of those I was able to witness while she remained in command of this body. This was something that remained untouched in the depths of her consciousness until this moment, when it arose unbidden, only to vanish when I returned to awareness.

My mind feels slow and sluggish, as though I just emerged from a deep sleep. But I was not asleep—at least, I don't believe so. I was lost to my thoughts, worrying about what is happening with the Grand Regent and the other De Gofroy, wondering how to thwart Osahi's designs. In spite of the late hour and my tiredness, my mind was frenetic. I could not sleep.

But my thoughts began to wander, as they do, and I soon gave in to the temptation of memory, which is, more and more, my only solace in this place. The memory that came was not my own.

Impossible.

I probe the corners of my mind, the dark places where my consciousness seems to dissipate, to be replaced by…something. A void? Laila? Who is to say. She is not present, though. I cannot feel her awareness, as I did when she reigned over me. Where then did this memory come from?

"It had to come from somewhere," I say in an angry voice.

I clap my hands over my mouth, realizing my mistake too late. If Meredith is watching, as I suspect she is, awaiting Laila's return, I cannot let her know that something so inexplicable has happened. She will try to encourage it. To bring about her return.

You're losing your damn mind, I tell myself, and wonder as I do if I have said it aloud again. It sounds like a shout in my mind. I can hear its echoes reverberating within.

To stop my spiraling mania and to calm both my body

and mind, I get up from bed and take a shower, letting the water wash me clean. When I emerge, my panic has subsided but my mind is still abuzz with thought, and I decide to go for a walk. Better to put myself to use than to lose myself to despair, I reason.

I dress hurriedly, though I don't know why, and leave my quarters, hesitating for a moment beside Meredith's door to listen to see if she is awake. I hear nothing, but know better than to assume. Rather than taking the elevator, I take the stairs down, hoping if nothing else to tire myself. At each level I get off and wander around, looking for signs of life and find none. The corridors are dark and still in the way that so many others on campus are. The Hierarchy once inhabited these quarters, but they are all gone now, fleeing with Osahi, or turned into half-things by the Acolytes.

A thought occurs to me as I explore. The Grand Regent must have transfer equipment nearby, perhaps not on the campus, but somewhere in the vicinity. If the Travelers raid the tower, he will want a means of escape close at hand. And the Acolytes will need some way to come here and take away the half-things to reapply the tamps. The suppressants only work for so long, as I know.

I decide I need to find the transfer equipment, the Grand Regent's escape route. If things go as I fear they will, I will need to make use of them. Osahi will wipe me clean as soon as he has the chance, so I need to be ready.

Ten of the eleven stories below the Grand Regent's floor are empty. The second story is not. The base of the tower is larger than the top floors, with the bottom two floors connecting to buildings on either side of the tower. Away from the bank of elevators, the second floor opens into what once was a large sitting area, at the center of which is an opening providing a view of the ground floor and an escalator and stairway leading up to the second. Both floors have large windows that provide a clear view of the surrounding campus. The hallways leading to the tower are broad and open, so anyone positioned here will have a clear view of all possible approaches.

This is where Osahi has positioned his people. He can track anyone who enters or leaves the tower, unless they do so by the underground tunnels that Laila came through. I suspect he has ways of seeing what goes on there as well, even if the Watchers who stand guard around the campus ultimately control them. Whatever arrangement exists between them, allowing Osahi and his people to be present on the campus when almost no other whole person is allowed near the Grand Regent must be a guarded and wary one on both sides.

The uneasiness of that relationship is apparent here in the encampment Osahi has established. Most of his people are in bed asleep in some of the side rooms, but there are guards standing watch at the windows and at the corridors, pulse weapons at hand. They do not seem surprised to see me as I emerge from the stairwell. Osahi is not visible, but De Vroes is busy in the midst of stacks of equipment arranged in one of the corners away from any windows or corridors. I recognize various Society implements that I used in my time as a Watcher, including, I am thrilled to see, transfer boxes.

De Vroes looks up at my approach. None of those standing watch move to intercept me. I am clearly not seen as a threat to anything they are doing here. Which is probably true, I am forced to admit.

The Acolyte gives me a grim smile. "What did you think of the show?"

"The Grand Regent was certainly impressed. My own feelings don't matter. I'm only there for decoration."

De Vroes turn his attention back to the piece of equipment he was working with. I do not recognize it and cannot see enough of it from where I stand to know what it is. He is an Acolyte, though, and that alone makes me uneasy.

"What does he want?" I say.

De Vroes does not look up. "You know the answer to that."

"To control the Grand Regent."

The Acolyte laughs. "No, that isn't it at all. Look at those suits he wears. The airs he puts on. He's never wanted to be in the shadows. That's where he was put because he was useful. Because that's what he's good at. What he wants is to be Grand Regent."

"He is not an easy man to remove," I say. "Many have tried."

"True. But he's banished his hatchet man. And he has no idea how vulnerable he is. The Watchers are getting restless. The Church is hemorrhaging faithful. You've seen this place. Things can't continue this way."

I shrug. What he says is true. And yet I cannot believe it will be so simple for Osahi to make himself Grand Regent. The Order will never accept it.

"What about your kind? They will have their say in things too."

"They will go along with whoever lets them continue with their work," De Vroes says, with a shake of his head. "Molijc encouraged them, fostered them and created a monster."

"Is that why you left?" I say.

De Vroes hesitates, looking over the equipment and tools before him. "There were a few in the guild who disagreed with what we were doing. I was one of them. But I haven't left the guild. I work with Osahi because I believed he would work to stop the worst of our abuses."

Here he looks at me, and I flinch. It is hard to think of oneself as the plaything of the Acolytes, yet that is what I am. And will be for some time yet, I fear.

When I recover myself, I realize that he used the past tense when talking of what he believed Osahi would do. Intriguing. "You don't believe in Osahi anymore?" I say. A challenge.

Again De Vroes hesitates. "I do. But I don't trust him

completely anymore. He's so near to what he's wanted for so long. People will compromise themselves completely and justify it because their goal is so tantalizingly close."

"You think the Acolytes will offer him a deal."

He shrugs, looking around as though he thinks we are being listened to. "If they think that Molijc is no longer a tenable Grand Regent and that Osahi will work with them, they may."

"The Watchers don't trust Osahi," I say. "They won't like the idea of him being Grand Regent, I can tell you that. Lasinha never trusted him."

"Things can change. Ideas, too. Lasinha is banished."

"What do you know about that?" I say, angling myself so that I can see the rest of the floor. Osahi's people remain focused on their tasks, ignoring De Vroes and I. Yet he seems jumpy, although perhaps I am reading my own roiling emotions onto him. He is certainly sharing more with me than I expected. But then, I am of no consequence to any of them. I do not matter.

"I don't know what happened. The Grand Regent claimed he banished him, but I'm not sure whether to believe that or not. Maybe he got a conscience, like Laila and Osahi."

He looks pointedly at me, and I flinch again.

"I have no problem sleeping at night," I say.

"You should," De Vroes says. "We all should. And the fact that you're here now, at this time of night, says to me that maybe you feel the same way."

It does not. But I do not tell him that.

9

Days pass unchanging, the tower and the campus feeling more and more empty. An absence that is spreading to envelop me. I develop a routine, more to stave off my despair and my sense that any chance I had at rescuing myself has slipped away. Mornings I traverse the campus, exploring those buildings that I have not yet entered, looking for something, anything that might help me. When I am done with that, I go to the borders of the campus and observe the Order keeping their watch until the changing of the guard.

I rarely eat; I am rarely hungry. My whole being feels as though it is vanishing. Laila's memories do not return, but I am too afraid to go back to my own, lest I trigger more to come forth. Only when I am absent-minded, distracted, do they emerge, in fragments and pieces that I hurriedly shove away. I remain in the present, this unending blankness. This nightmare.

Better to have been left Joseph Aurellano, a half-thing with no memory, watched over by a broken woman.

She watches over me still, though only halfheartedly, rarely leaving her quarters. We are both aware that the end nears. Osahi will succeed in removing the Grand Regent.

What will become of us then, I do not know.

In the depths of another sleepless night, there is a knock at my door. Meredith stands there, a knowing grin on her face.

"Can't sleep?" she says.

I ignore her question and answer with one my own. "What do you want?"

"I want to be free of this madness," she says, in an offhand kind of way, as though she is talking about changing her hairstyle. "But I'm not the one who wants you. The Grand Regents summons you."

I blink in surprise. Now that the Grand Regent has a new plaything, I assume I am not needed to listen to his ramblings. Perhaps he has grown tired of the De Gofroy already. I follow Meredith, not bothering to make myself more presentable. I doubt it will matter. Whatever the Grand Regent has to say, my presence will be enough. My appearance and everything else about me is inconsequential. He may as well summon Morris or another of the half-things—whatever is left of his wife—as talk to me. In a way he has, and perhaps he does not see the difference between us. We are all vessels in his mind.

"Why don't you just leave?" I say to Meredith as we near the half-Morris standing vigil by the door to the audience chamber. "I know why I have to stay. I need her gone. I need my body back. But I don't understand why you would bother. None of them will ever trust you again. Least of all her."

I am rewarded with a flinch, the first sign I have seen of her façade collapsing. She recovers quickly, not breaking stride, giving me a mocking smile.

"I'm waiting for her to tell me that," she says. "Even he wants her back, you know. That was the deal with Osahi. He didn't want you. You're what he got stuck with."

I swallow and do not respond, striding past Morris as he opens the door. Meredith doesn't bother to follow me into the audience chamber. Only her laughter accompanies me as I approach the dais where the Grand Regent sits. He is lost in thought, his face lined with worry, and does not notice me. I cough to let him know I am there, and he glances down, a vacant expression on his face for a moment, until he recognizes me.

"Aeida," he says in a soft voice. He sounds weak, as though stricken by some ailment. "Always a faithful vessel. It is good to have you near in these times of tribulation."

"It is good to be here," I say. "I will serve the faith in whatever way I can."

"Of course." He smiles, his eyes distant again. "Such tribulations. But I feel we are getting nearer. Nearer by the moment. De Gofroy has been the source of many revelations, but his true self still escapes me."

I purse my lips, knowing I must speak but dreading doing so. "Do you trust him?"

"Who?" the Grand Regent says, glancing at me as though surprised that I am there. "De Gofroy? Of course he is not the De Gofroy I knew, though he is very similar, in ways that I would not have thought possible. But yes, I trust him. Of course I do. The differences between him and the De Gofroy I knew are illuminating. Most illuminating. He will be the catalyst to bring me closer to De Gofroy's true being, of that I am certain. But it is difficult. A struggle."

By the end, he is musing to himself again. I might as well be one of the Mayan codices hanging on the wall, stolen from who knows what universe. I cough again, to draw his attention to me and say, "He is Osahi's. You know that, Grand Regent. He is only here because of a deal he made with Osahi." And I tell him of what Laila overheard outside the house where Osahi hid the other De Gofroy.

The Grand Regent frowns, his cheeks going red with anger. "Osahi," he says. "Never to be trusted. This was our deal, you understand. He would give me Laila and this

De Gofroy he had procured, and I would agree to let him return to the faith. Have the Watchers stand down. He has held up his end of the bargain, no doubt. But I don't forget, Aeida. And I don't forgive betrayals of his kind. I let Laila talk me into letting Osahi back into the faith once. I shall not make the same mistake again."

I am forced to look away from the Grand Regent as he stares at me, the intensity of his gaze still so overwhelming to me. It cows me, even as I can hear Laila's laughter in my head at the idea. To her, he was just Dejian Molijc, a man with more faults than most. To me, he is the Grand Regent. He always will be. I cannot abandon him now, even though I fear that remaining at his side will destroy me. In that, I suspect I am no different than Meredith. We have both gone too far down this road to turn back.

Only Lasinha could turn me aside. I would follow him…but I fear he has joined the Grand Regent's menagerie of half-things.

Though I know I am tempting fate, I press the Grand Regent again. I must do so, for it is clear no one else will. "It is good that you realize the danger Osahi represents," I begin.

"I know more than you ever will the danger he represents," the Grand Regent says, leaning forward and pointing a finger at my chest.

"Of course, Grand Regent," I say, trying to recover my momentum as the blood drains from my face. "But… has it occurred to you that Osahi may have told this De Gofroy what to say to you? To try to make you act against your interests. And the faith's."

The Grand Regent waves a dismissive hand at me. "You think I, of all people, am not aware of what is best for the faith? I am the faith's greatest vessel. Its most important. My connection with De Gofroy's true self. The visions." He frowns, seeming to lose his train of thought. "De Gofroy is essential to what the faith needs. It needs my connection to him. Why have so many people left:

71

because they question that connection. So Osahi can play his little tricks and try to connive his way to this chair all he wants. I am ready for him."

"I'm glad to hear it, Grand Regent," I say. "Still. We should prepare ourselves. Osahi has a base on the second floor of this tower. There is nothing to stop him—"

"I am aware of his little fortress. Do not think I am unaware." His voice echoes around the room and his eyes bulge out. He calms himself and continues in a level voice. "Who do you think allowed him to be there? Who, Aeida? Don't worry yourself about these matters. They are not your concern. Everything is proceeding as I intend it. You must put your mind to searching Laila's memories. There are secrets there…"

He trails off, looking off into the distance again, as though he has forgotten that I am there. I wait for a time to see if he will say anything further, but he does not.

"I will, Grand Regent," I say at last.

He nods distractedly, not even turning in my direction, chasing some thought. I watch him a moment longer before I turn and go.

10

A crack of thunder awakens me. *An attack* is my first thought. *The Society. What do I do?*

A second low rumble follows the first, and I recognize what it is as the fog of sleep begins to dissipate. I stumble out of bed and go to the window, where I see that morning is near, the red of dawn just touching the western horizon. Darkness still holds sway here, though, the entire campus murky and obscure. Rain begins to pelt the window as lightning scorches the horizon, making me flinch.

I watch the storm for a time, mesmerized by it. Though I have spent some time in Western Canada, in the other universe, I am not well versed in its seasons. As best I can determine, it is spring now, the empty boughs of the trees gradually filling with buds of green. A thunderstorm at this time of the year must be a rare occurrence. As I watch, I cannot help but feel it is significant, even as I know it isn't. It is only weather, after all, a passing storm that will vanish in an hour. Yet I can't help feeling it is a harbinger of sorts. But of what?

Eventually I grow tired of watching the storm and try to return to bed and to sleep. I do for a time, or at least I slip into something akin to it. A sort of hazy reverie, where my body feels light and pinpricked with sleep and my thoughts are absent. The rumbles of thunder grow closer, and more cacophonous, and then quieten as the storm passes by.

I start awake as the storm ends and even the patter of rain on the window ceases. There was a voice or…something that brought me from my half-sleeping state. I blink and look around, fully awake, my heart pounding with fear, and my hands clenched, ready to fight. But who?

I calm myself by degrees, convincing myself that I am alone. Though never entirely. She is still within me somewhere. And the more I think about it, the more certain I am that the thought that awakened me was hers. It has the feeling of a memory, springing unbidden from the depths of my mind, something like my recollection of her rendezvous with Morris. But I cannot remember now what this new memory was, unlike that first.

It is terrifying to think that my thoughts may not be my own. That Laila can operate without my being aware of her. Though I have no proof of that just yet. A memory is just that and nothing more. I am not doing anything at her command. Not yet, anyway.

What is clear is that I need to be on my guard against her. I may not have as much time as I hoped. Certainly I can afford to wait no longer. I will have to try to convince the Grand Regent to remove her from my mind, but I have no idea how.

Sleep eludes me for what remains of the night, and finally I arise as light streams in through the window where I forgot to draw the curtains. After I head to the floor below, where there is a small kitchen that is somehow always well stocked, and have some breakfast, I find myself at loose ends. As I ponder my next steps, paralyzed by an inability to see a way forward and a desperate need to do something, anything before I lose my chance. Meredith comes down to the kitchen and helps herself to some of the coffee that I made.

She studies me with her usual ironic detachment as she sips from her cup. "Trouble sleeping, Aeida?"

It seems like two questions at once. Not just asking if I was restless, but also inquiring whether I am, in fact, still Aeida. After my fears of several hours before, it feels a little too on the nose. *What does she know?* But, of course, she knows nothing, I remind myself. She only hopes.

"You know the answer to that question," I say. "I would think by now you could find better things to do with your evenings than watch me."

"You'd be surprised," she says.

"I still don't understand why you stay here," I say. "There's really nothing left here for you. Just memories."

"You'd be surprised," she says again, smiling this time.

It is a disquieting grin, and I have to look away.

"But I could ask you the same thing," she says. "Why stay? The Grand Regent will never give you what you want. He doesn't want you. He wants Laila. And if Osahi manages his little coup, then you'll be lucky to survive. Better to go somewhere else and see if you can find someone else to do what you want. Maybe the Seekers will lend a hand. They seem to be friendly toward you."

"Laila is the one they're interested in," I say.

"She is the one we're all interested in. You are just a vessel for her. And a nuisance otherwise."

I grimace, my face hot with anger. Yet I cannot deny what she has said. It is true. I do not matter to any of these people. Even the Grand Regent, who I have served faithfully and done unspeakable things for. Which means it is time for me to forgot all of them and see to myself. While I still have time.

I get to my feet and, with a dismissive nod to Meredith, leave the kitchen and go upstairs.

The half-Morris looks blankly at me as I approach the door to the Grand Regent's chambers. For a moment I am unsure if he even recognizes me. Will he stop me, I wonder, if I am not with Meredith or if the Grand Regent has not summoned me? What will I do then? There is only one way to find out.

I nod at him. "I'm here to see the Grand Regent," I say in what I hope is an officious tone.

His blank stare continues and he makes no move either to open the door or to intercept me. I return his stare, waiting for some signal as to what I should do. There is none, and at length I simply open the door and enter the audience room. Morris does not even glance in my direction as I close the door behind me.

The audience room is empty, and for a moment I linger there, overcome by a sort of awe. There are the calendar pieces, with their intersecting long counts demonstrating the connectedness of the universes. Carved into the ceiling is the hunab ku, the symbol of the one true universe and our true selves moving through the other universes.

"You are my other I," I whisper. It is something De Gofroy once wrote, which always seemed to explain the faith to me. Now, with the arrival of the other De Gofroy, it feels ominous.

I pass from the audience room to the next chamber, where the Grand Regent met with Meredith, Osahi, and I. The room is empty, and I pause again at its center, where the hunab ku is inscribed upon the floor and where the Grand Regent prays and conducts Protocols upon himself. This is all the holiest of ground for me, places I heard about only from Lasinha, or read about in De Gofroy or Molijc's books. It feels wrong for me to be here alone, unescorted. I am a lowly sub-Regent, after all.

But I press on through the various rooms, all of which are empty, with little appearance of somebody actually occupying them and living here. Where does the Grand Regent spend his time? Even the bed in his vast quarters appears unslept in. As I go from room to room, I begin to feel that something is very wrong. At first it is a niggling sensation that I brush aside, but as I see room after empty room, with none of the usual detritus of human activity, I find myself wondering what can be going on. What is the Grand Regent doing?

It is only when I retrace my steps back to the audience chamber that I remember there is a small study just aside it, where De Gofroy once kept the files on all the faithful, which Laila stole. The door that led there is gone, or at least it is not where it was in Laila's memory, from what I can recall of it. But a vague suspicion leads me to investigate the wall more closely, and I soon uncover its outlines.

The mechanism to unlock it takes a little longer to discover, but I know enough about how the Order to know how they would construct a door like this. When I do manage to open it, I discover the Grand Regent and the other De Gofroy, huddled together in deep discussion.

"Aeida," the Grand Regent says, looking up in surprise at the open door and me standing in the threshold. "Come in. Join us."

De Gofroy frowns and glances at the Grand Regent, but says nothing. I step within, pulling the door closed behind me, and receive an approving nod from the Grand Regent. There is no chair for me to sit on, so I stand by the doorway and study the room. A quick glance tells me that this is where the Grand Regent is effectively living now.

There is a cot stuffed in the corner by the safe that once held De Gofroy's files and now presumably holds Molijc's. The bookshelves and desk—which, along with the two chairs the men are sitting in, occupy most of the space in the room—are littered with plates and cups. There is the smell of stale food and coffee starting to grow mold. The light is dim and the one window has the blinds drawn tight.

It all speaks to a life lived in isolation, meals eaten in seclusion and nights spent alone. But what has driven the Grand Regent here? The campus is protected by his Watchers and Morris stands watch at the door, presumably ready to block any trespassers. Where is Laila's body? Where are all the others who he summons to his audiences? They must be kept somewhere, yet I have seen no sign of them anywhere on campus.

The Grand Regent appears not to notice what is drawing my eyes, but De Gofroy follows my gaze carefully, his frown deepening. He does not want me here, that much is obvious.

His discomfort sets me at ease, and I turn to the Grand Regent. "Thank you for seeing me. I apologize for the intrusion, but I have something of grave importance to discuss with you."

The Grand Regent gives me another distant, imperious nod, as though whatever matters I wish to talk about are beneath him. "In due time, Aeida, in due time. But while you are here, I want you to listen to what De Gofroy just told me. Utterly fascinating."

De Gofroy shifts uncomfortably in his chair, glancing from me to the Grand Regent, as though looking for some way to escape answering the request put before him. Finding none, he says, "I was telling the Grand Regent about my work studying the Maya. I wrote several books on the matter. I discovered if one looks at their glyphs carefully, you can see tales of ancient peoples bringing sacred knowledge to the Mayans, who codified it for their descendants to discover."

The Grand Regent looks at me significantly, and I nod, opening my mouth and closing it.

De Gofroy clears his throat. "It seems obvious now that I know about the other universes and all *this*." He waves his hand about to encompass the faith. "Well, it seems obvious that the Mayans were brought this information by others who could cross the universes.

Ancient beings who understood the nature of the universes and our disparate beings."

The Grand Regent leans forward, excited. "De Gofroy—the other De Gofroy—speculated as much in some of his early works."

"Speculated and rejected," I say in a hard voice. "The idea does not stand up to any of the archaeological records. The Mayans received their insight the same way De Gofroy did. The same way you yourself did. They were able to perceive the true nature of the universes. Just as the best among us can do so without the Protocols."

The other De Gofroy offers a shrug. "I am only learning of your faith. I am hardly an expert."

"Indeed," I say, the back of my neck growing hot. "Have you taken the Protocols? Or the Pre-scripts?"

He shakes his head, looking to the Grand Regent, who puts a finger to his lips thoughtfully.

Sensing an opening, I press my advantage. "And these books of yours, what were they? Histories? Fiction?"

De Gofroy shifts in his chair, clearly uncomfortable. "As I said to the Grand Regent, they were religious texts of a sort. Not entirely dissimilar from what the De Gofroy here wrote. In my universe, there was something called Mayanism, a sort of new-age religion. My books appealed to adherents of those ideas."

"But you didn't believe them," I say.

"Of course I did," De Gofroy says. "Why else would I write them? They were speculations that I see now were ultimately wrong. But clearly I was thinking along the same lines as my counterpart in this universe."

"With none of his insight. What did you do before that?"

De Gofroy again turns to the Grand Regent, looking for help to end this interrogation, but there is none forthcoming. The real De Gofroy fought in the Society wars that tore apart this universe. When they were over, he, like many others, threw aside all the old faiths and beliefs of the one-universe world and went in search of truth. The truth the Travelers were hiding from them. But this De Gofroy did not fight in any wars, was not scarred by the crumbling of the edifices upon which all civilization had been constructed. He is a dilettante. A liar. A scoundrel. I can sense it.

"I have always been something of a scholar. A seeker of truths. Obviously I did not gain the insights of my counterpart, but in my defense, this Society of Travelers did not occupy my universe. I was left to fumble alone in the darkness. I practiced mysticism, Aleister Crowley, that sort of thing. Joined communes of various colors. Free love, anarcho-syndicalist. Even dabbled some in Dianetics."

"Wrote books on it all, I imagine. Led seminars."

"I have always been happy to share what meager insight I have gained in this existence."

"Anything to earn a dollar?" I say, giving him a sneering smile.

He winces. "I suppose that is one way to look at it. I would prefer—"

"And what were you doing before Osahi dug you up?"

De Gofroy will not look at me. "I was… Well, my seeking led me to a study of medicine. Natural medicine. Ancient remedies. It was a natural fit, after all my investigations into the Maya. There are herbs and plants that can cure any known disease, you know. Water even has great power."

"Leeches, too," I say in disgust. "You were a charlatan, in other words. Peddling naturopath quackery to whoever would buy it."

"I can see how it would seem that way to you, but I assure you that was not the case. I believed in the power of these ancient remedies, just as I believed in the ancient teachings of the Maya. I brought this understanding to people who shared a like mind."

"You were a charlatan, profiting off the backs of the

credulous. It is people like you who give our faith a bad name in this universe and others. Our beliefs have scientific backing. The Protocols have been well researched. Unlike whatever nonsense you are spouting."

De Gofroy's face darkens, but he does not take my bait. "I can see that now, of course. Perhaps, on some level, I always knew that. But I had no choice. My works had stopped selling, you understand. I had a family to feed. An ex-wife. The sorts of burdens one collects along the path of life. Anyway. None of that matters now. I am here and I hope I can help the Grand Regent find his truth. As I said, I have always been a seeker."

"A seeker," I say, looking at the Grand Regent, who is frowning, his eyes narrowed. "A grifter is more like it. What other scams did you run?"

De Gofroy stands, deciding he has suffered my abuse for long enough. "I am no grifter. I am a seeker of truth, with the courage to be wrong and to continue my search to understand the universe. That search has led me here to help the Grand Regent as I may. But I do not need to listen to your insults."

He storms out of the study, leaving the secret door ajar. I can hear his steps echoing across the audience room. The Grand Regent is looking at me with a stern and unreadable expression.

"Thank you, Aeida," he says with a nod, as though he summoned me for this very purpose. "You are a faithful vessel."

It is a dismissal. On reflex, I turn and go, closing the door behind me, leaving the Grand Regent to his hidden study. It is only when I am outside the audience chamber, looking into Morris' empty eyes, that it occurs to me that I did not do what I set out to when I entered the room. I wanted to confront the Grand Regent, to convince him somehow to free me from Laila.

Yet once I was in the study, face to face with that pretender, I was drawn to interrogate him. To find the chink in his armor. That was my own compulsion, I feel certain, my own desire to protect the Grand Regent from Osahi's plot. But everything about the Grand Regent—his expression and attitude throughout, his allowing me to go on attacking the man he saw as central to the faith's survival, the way he thanked me at the end—suggested he was not surprised by what I was doing. He expected it and he wanted me to do it.

But how could he know that I would? The thought, and the vacancy behind Morris' expression, shake me to the core. I return to my quarters, no longer certain that my thoughts are at all my own.

11

I return to my room, shaken and uncertain, wanting to gather my thoughts, such as they are, before deciding my next step. But my mind will not allow me to do so. My thoughts keep slipping away into paranoid fantasies where I imagine Meredith creeping into my quarters at night to drug me with some Acolyte concoction that will make me act at the Grand Regent's command. It is a foolish notion. Meredith, if she could, would work to bring Laila back, and so would the Grand Regent.

Despite the few slips and oddities—memories that have no origin—I cannot sense her presence. It is not like before. Not at all.

I do not feel reassured, though, just the opposite. I feel as though I am waiting for the worst to happen, whatever that may be. Expecting it. This is the time to act.

My meeting with the Grand Regent having proved less than useful, I decide to head downstairs to see what Osahi and his minions are up to. I have no plan in mind and simply hope a course of action presents itself somehow. There is a clawing at my chest as I descend, the passages of my airways narrowing, and when I close my eyes, I can feel the walls closing in. There is no escaping this. I will be here until the end, whatever that is.

When I arrive on the second floor, Osahi is yelling at the other De Gofroy, his voice carrying up the stairwell.

"What the fuck did I tell you? Never. Never leave the Grand Regent's side. No matter what. You need to be there."

De Gofroy responds in an angry voice, almost unrecognizable from the one he uses with the Grand Regent. "The Asian kid was asking questions. Too many of them. And I got tired of answering them."

I pause by the elevators to listen to the conversation further, earning a glare from the woman on watch.

Osahi sounds even more irate, his voice hoarse with anger. "Of course he was asking questions. He knows we're up to something. Your part in this is to sit there and answer those questions. Whatever they may be. Under no circumstances are you to leave the Grand Regent alone."

The woman looks as though she is about to announce my presence to Osahi, so I start forward, moving from the bank of elevators down the corridor to where it opens out into the encampment they have constructed. Osahi and De Gofroy are standing in the center of the room glaring at each other. Both turn at my approach, Osahi's rage vanishing from his face in an instant, replaced by a guarded disdain, while De Gofroy only seems to grow more irate.

"You see. What the hell is this kid doing everywhere? He's following me around. You're supposed to be controlling this situation."

"I am," Osahi says, in a tone that says he does not need to hear anything more from De Gofroy. "Now get upstairs and do your fucking job."

De Gofroy looks as though he wants to argue further, but he clamps his mouth shut and starts toward the elevators. As he passes me, moving at an ambling shuffle that I know will make Osahi even more furious, he shoots me a pointed glare. I smile and walk up to Osahi, the grin still on my face.

"What shithole universe did you drag that grifter up from?" I say, in an innocent voice.

"Spare me," Osahi says, looking at me with disgust. De Vroes approaches and hovers nearby, looking warily between us.

I laugh. "You may have him convinced you can control this, but we both know you can't. The Grand Regent is going to see through De Gofroy eventually. I'll see to that. And even if he doesn't, the Watchers will not just let you put the faith in peril."

Osahi shakes his head. "He is the one who has put the faith in peril. Don't think I have forgotten the part you played in that, either. And don't worry about the Watchers. We have an understanding."

What sort of understanding? is what I want to ask, but I do not. He will only lie. That is probably true of all he has said to me up to this point. Lies and bluster and obfuscation to keep me off balance.

Before I can respond, De Vroes makes his presence known to Osahi and the two of them lean in close and whisper across each other's shoulders while I watch. I can barely make out any of their murmurs, though I can see De Vroes' lips and I am certain I make out the words "tamp" and "orb." Who is he working on? I am both repulsed and compelled by the thought. I need the Acolytes or De Vroes, and yet I cannot stomach the thought of them mucking about in my head again.

Their murmurs grow more and more heated. My presence, once a comfortable nuisance, easily ignored, becomes awkward and finally intolerable. Osahi turns to glare at me, and when I don't leave, he does, shouting over his shoulder at De Vroes.

"Do it. I'm not discussing the matter any further. Why can't anybody just do what they're told?"

De Vroes and I watch him disappear into one of the side rooms before turning to each other. The renegade

Acolyte has a troubled expression and looks exhausted. I imagine I must look the same.

"Problems, problems, problems," I say with a shrug.

"This will not end well," De Vroes says. "Not at all."

I look at him curiously. "More doubts about the great leader?"

He looks at me with a bitter smile. "It is as I feared. He can taste it now. He is so close that he will do whatever they want, so long as he gets to sit on that throne. But what will be left when he does?"

"Nothing," I say, my voice filled with a sudden emotion I cannot place. "There is nothing left now."

De Vroes looks at me with a raised eyebrow and nods.

I return upstairs, still unable to see a path forward, and more unsure than ever about what to do. Osahi's plan is the problem. I cannot fathom it. He is waiting for something, but I don't know what. If I knew what else he was doing... But in spite of De Vroes' apparent doubts in his master, he will not confide that in me. He knows I am not to be trusted and has chosen which side he will stand on, just as I have. We will die on those hills, sacrificed by the men we put our faith in.

Well, the man I put my faith in is not here. He is banished or gone apostate, who is to say? Lasinha I know and can trust. Everyone else here is against me, except perhaps the Grand Regent, but he appears so lost. How can he allow himself to be so seduced by so obvious a fool as De Gofroy?

The man is a huckster, nothing more. His job is obviously to keep the Grand Regent occupied while whatever Osahi and his people are trying to do comes to fruition. It must be an alliance with the Acolytes, given De Vroes' misgivings. The Watchers will never trust Osahi, I feel certain. They will never go to his side. Even with Lasinha banished, they will not.

These thoughts are still on my mind as I emerge from

my long climb up the stairwell to see De Gofroy sitting with Morris before the Grand Regent's door. It is odd to see them there like that, arms slung around each other like old bosom friends. Neither of them notices me as I linger by the doorway.

"They said I was stealing people's money, but they didn't understand at all," De Gofroy is saying to Morris, who is watching him with his blank eyes. "It was never about the money. Never. It was about trying to help people. Trying to understand our universes. This De Gofroy, though, he was better than I was. That much is clear. Better than I by a long shot. Look at what he built."

He looks around, holding up his hand, and Morris follows his gesture like a cat fascinated by a toy. Both of them see me at the same time, though it takes some time for my presence to register in their faces.

"You again," De Gofroy says, his eyes narrowing. There is the slightest of slurs to his voice that I had not noticed before. Was it there when he was with Osahi?

"I have a name," I say.

"Indeed," he says, as though confirming to Morris that I do possess one.

"Shouldn't you be guarding the Grand Regent?" I say to Morris.

A look of guilt passes across his face, the first genuinely human expression of emotion I have seen from him since I came here. He scrambles to his feet and stands, stiff and erect, by the door, not looking at De Gofroy or I.

"Leave him be," De Gofroy says angrily. "Hasn't he suffered enough?"

"He's been punished for his apostasy. Now he is a faithful vessel. All of us know that we must do what is required."

De Gofroy shakes his head, getting unsteadily to his feet. He nearly falls over once he is upright and has to lean on Morris for support.

"Why any of you do anything for that man is beyond

me," he says, looking in my direction, trying and failing to focus his gaze upon me. "He is a madman. Plain and simple."

"He is the Grand Regent of the Church of Regents," I say in a calm voice.

De Gofroy laughs. "Such a grand title. High Regent. Grand Regent. Ooh la la. Unbelievable what he built here."

"*He*," I say, "understood the true nature of the universes. He knew the importance of the struggle that lay before us for the fate of ourselves and the sacrifices would have to be made."

"Did he now? Seems to me only some are making sacrifices. That madman in there is just doing whatever crazy thing pops in his mind. And you are following along like good little sheep to the slaughterhouse."

I give him a knowing smile, though his words make me uneasy. "You don't know anything about the faith or its tenets. You don't understand why we would gladly do this. Gladly sacrifice ourselves. We know this flesh is just a vessel and our true selves lie elsewhere."

De Gofroy pushes himself away from Morris and teeters on the edge of falling before righting himself. He was not this far gone with Osahi, which means he must have taken something once he left. What in the world, I wonder, could he be using to get himself this high, this quickly? His eyes gradually come into focus on me.

"I don't know the faith, it's true," he says. "But I know me. I know what I would do and I know what I would say. I never had any special insight. I just borrowed things from here and there. This De Gofroy did the same thing, I guarantee. You think he came up with all this mumbo jumbo on his own? Somebody gave this to him."

"He is not like you," I say stiffly, my lungs again feeling as though they are being squeezed empty.

"But we are so similar in so many ways, aren't we?" he says with an impish grin. "I wish I could have built this

88

here in my world. I would have been like him and made sure I wasn't around when the debt came due, though. All of you would be wise to do the same."

I stiffen at his words. "De Gofroy gave his earthly vessel to the faith. Now his soul awaits us, to guide us to the other universes."

"Like I said, don't wait around for the check to come due. That's one place where he definitely had more insight than me, I'll give you that."

He laughs again at the expression on my face, before turning to Morris. "Now, if you'll excuse me, I have to attend to your Grand Regent."

"What is Osahi's plan?" I say, deciding I have nothing else to lose. "What is this all about?"

De Gofroy chuckles and winks at me over his shoulder. "You think Osahi tells me what his plan is? Don't be stupid. I'm just supposed to keep the Grand Regent occupied, which isn't difficult, let me tell you. He doesn't need an audience to ramble on about vessels or whatever."

"And what do you get out of this? Why bother if you hate it all so much?"

"Like I said, kid, your De Gofroy was smarter than me. He got out before the check came due. I'll be paying for a long, long time."

He looks at Morris, who opens the door for him, and with a friendly wave at us both, the other De Gofroy disappears within.

12

The next evening, just after I have gone to bed, Meredith knocks on my door and informs me the Grand Regent wishes to see me again. I have been unable to forget my last conversation with the other De Gofroy. His talk of debts coming due has frightened me more than even I realized. We, all of us, have debts to be paid here. I am paying mine in some ways, and in others I have not begun to.

The confirmation that De Gofroy is merely a tool to distract the Grand Regent is of little comfort. It still does not explain what Osahi is planning to do. He is putting something in place to remove both Molijc and the Watchers and replace them with himself and his people. With Lasinha gone, and no strong hand to guide the Order, perhaps he thinks he can get the Acolytes' acquiescence. But the Watchers will not go quietly.

Nor will the Grand Regent. I find him alone in the audience room, a pensive look on his face. Something, I think, has changed.

"Aeida," he says, nodding at me, but not saying anything else.

I stand before him, below the dais where he sits upon

his throne, waiting for him to speak, but he does not. After letting the silence grow, I wonder if he has forgotten my presence and decide I must speak.

"You summoned me, Grand Regent?"

He looks at me, distracted and confused, his eyes slowly coming into focus. "Ah yes. Aeida. Strange days, are they not?"

"They are," I say.

"Difficult ones as well. I wonder if you have found anything in Laila's memories. They are key to this, I am certain. There is something there. The Society is doing something to thwart my efforts to reach the true De Gofroy. I have talked and talked with this other one on so many matters, to no effect. He is quite like him, though, quite like him. In so many ways."

I hesitate a moment, wetting my lips. "Perhaps it is he who is the trouble, not the Society."

The Grand Regent appears to ponder this, before shaking his head. "No, I do not think so. He knows so little of the faith and all these intrigues. It is all foreign to him."

"I don't know, Grand Regent. How long was he in Osahi's encampment? How much did Osahi prepare him for this moment? He wanted him to have your ear for a reason."

The Grand Regent stands up from his throne and wanders over to study one of the Mayan calendar wheels set into the wall. "It is remarkable that he studied the Maya, just as our De Gofroy did. I wonder if others in other universes are the same. I would think so. Their minds were bent along the same path. They all understood the importance of what the Maya had discovered, and what we had lost along the way. It was only our De Gofroy who was able to make the true connections, to reach across the universes to his other selves."

I resist the urge to sigh. The Grand Regent has been seduced by this charlatan, as Osahi hoped he would be.

"He is unique among all the universes," I say.

"Indeed, Aeida," the Grand Regent says. He is lost in thought again.

As I watch the Grand Regent, looking as uncertain as I have ever seen him, I decide I have nothing left to lose.

"Grand Regent, I believe the problem is Osahi. He is working with that renegade Acolyte of his. I think they are doing things to De Gofroy. I saw him yesterday and he was not himself. He was not himself at all."

The Grand Regent's eyes narrow as he considers this. He turns to me. "What makes you think they have done something to him?"

"I overheard Osahi and the Acolyte speaking. They were talking about it."

"About what?" He is suddenly a commanding presence before me, his eyes flashing.

"The procedures. They were talking tamps and suppressants."

"And you are certain they were talking about De Gofroy?"

I give an evasive shrug. "I can't say for certain, Grand Regent. I didn't hear all that they said. But that was the inference I drew from the conversation."

"Did they say his name?"

"No."

The Grand Regent heaves a dissatisfied breath. "A supposition, then. You have no proof."

"But I saw De Gofroy yesterday," I say, insistent, even as I feel the ground slipping away beneath me. "He wasn't himself."

"Aeida, do you really think that I, of all people, would not recognize someone who the Acolytes had performed their procedures on?"

"I suppose not," I say, unable to conceal my disappointment.

The Grand Regent nods, satisfied. "No, I know what Osahi is up to, and it isn't that. You do not need to worry about him. His wings will be clipped soon enough. It is the Travelers. They are insidious."

"Yes, Grand Regent."

A cunning look comes over his face. "You are certain Laila's memories have yielded nothing?"

"I… Well…" I stumble over the words, thinking for a moment that I might lie, but worried that will only lead me into even more troubled waters.

"You fear her return," he says.

My mouth opens and closes, but no words come forth. I nod.

"Yes. It is understandable. And you fear that once she does, I will leave her in possession of your body. But that is not the case, Aeida, I assure you."

"Yes, Grand Regent."

"You don't believe me." He smiles. "I can't blame you for that. But I will show you that what I say is true."

I try to swallow, my mouth suddenly dry. The Grand Regent turns and motions toward the door leading into the rest of his quarters.

"You may come out now," he says imperiously.

The door opens and Ana emerges, a vacant half-smile upon her lips. "Aeida," she says, as she approaches.

The air goes from me, and I find it difficult to move, as I am mesmerized again by her beauty. She looks just the same as the last time I saw her, so heartbreakingly innocent. The confused look on her face as the Watchers burst into the room to seize me—while Lasinha watched, unsmiling, from the doorway—has never left me. It was only then I could admit to myself what I had done. The look on Lasinha's face said as much; it spoke of how unforgivable it was.

The Grand Regent is watching me carefully. "You see, Aeida? I am loyal to my faithful vessels."

I say nothing, unable to take my eyes away from Ana's. Desire throttles my veins, even as I tell myself not to be distracted by this temptation. It is clear that the Grand

Regent intends to stay upon whatever path he has set himself, even if it leads to his destruction. I cannot turn him aside, but I can at least save myself, so long as I do not allow myself to be seduced.

The Grand Regent turns to Ana. "You would like to go with Aeida, wouldn't you, Ana? You are a faithful vessel."

"Yes," she says.

"This is a show of my faith, Aeida, and that I will reward you if you succeed," he says, turning back to me. "Do not disappoint me. You need not fear Laila's return. I will restore you to yourself."

I still cannot speak. The world has gone still and all I can see is Ana.

"What do you say, Aeida?" the Grand Regent says.

I take my eyes from Ana at last and look at him. "I am your faithful vessel, Grand Regent."

He smiles, nods, and retreats to the study behind the hidden door, leaving me alone with Ana.

THREE

AFTEREFFECTS

13

I open my eyes to darkness. Form gradually becomes visible. The furniture in the room, the curtains on the window, the darkness beyond it, which is different in texture than the one within. I can feel the sheets tangled around this naked body, my skin sticky with sweat that has dried upon me. The thought makes me shudder and my arm brushes against Ana's back. She stirs in her sleep but does not wake.

Something tears deep inside me, a rot that builds and builds, and I run to the bathroom, making it to the toilet just in time to vomit. When I have emptied my stomach of all it contains, I remain there, leaning against the tub and sobbing quietly. I do not want to awaken Ana. I cannot face whatever of her is left. Is some part of her dimly aware of what she is being subjected to? I hope not. The thought is unbearable.

All of this is too horrifying to contemplate. And it is my fault. I failed her, failed to listen to her warnings, and allowed her to fall into Molijc's grasp. Aeida may have committed the crime against her, but I made it all possible with my neglect and my vanity that I was part of something universe-shaking and important. Central to its efforts, in fact. It made me blind to the carnage we were inflicting on so many. How many other Anas are there? How many Morrises?

To think I once believed we were in a war for the fate of the universe. Now I know the terrible truth. I have been face to face with it in those moments when I have peered from behind Aeida's blind eyes and seen what Molijc is. We have eaten ourselves to the bone. In our search for our true selves, we have rendered our selves immaterial. We are vessels and nothing more, to be used and cast aside. What kind of life is that?

Not one I wish to be living. If I could take hold of this body and leave, I would. Even if I had to spend the rest of my days in this false flesh, I would do so. Enough damage has been done, by me and by so many others, that to leave it behind would be so cleansing. But that is not my choice to make. Not yet.

When I have recovered enough, I get up and return to the bedroom. Despite myself, I watch Ana sleep, the overwhelming sadness and despair returning in full force. I cannot help her by standing here, though, so I begin to get dressed, fumbling about in the dark for my clothes. I don't know how much time I will have before Aeida returns— not long, I suspect. He is asleep, and when he awakens, I may disappear again, to lurk behind his thoughts, where he cannot see me.

The jangle of my belt as I slide it through the loops on my jeans awakens Ana. She sits up in bed and looks over at me, and I freeze in place.

"Aeida," she says, rubbing her eyes. "Is it time to get up?"

"No," I say, forcing my voice into Aeida's register. "Go back to sleep."

Ana smiles and lies back down, and soon I hear her breathing deepen. I wait for a few minutes to make sure she has returned to sleep before I slip out of the room. In the hallway, I pause, debating what to do and waiting to see if I can hear Meredith stirring in her quarters. It is difficult to be near her again as well, after being done with her and saying my goodbyes. I made my peace with that part of my past at the farmhouse in the other universe. At least I thought I did. Now Meredith is here again, waiting for me. It is not safe for me to be around her.

Hearing nothing, I set off down the corridor toward the Grand Regent's chambers. I don't know why I go there first. It is dangerous for me there—if Molijc is awake and sees me for who I am, who knows what he will do. But some instinct—or compulsion—leads me there, even as I tell myself to go elsewhere. In the end, it doesn't matter, I realize. There are no safe spaces here, nowhere for me to hide. Osahi, Molijc, Meredith, even Aeida in this very body. All will turn on me given the slightest chance.

Morris is at the door, standing watch—does he never sleep?—but he does not move or even glance at me as I go within. The lights are off in the audience chamber, and darkness continues to hold sway outside, but I know this place so well that I do not bother to turn them on. That would only alert Molijc, who is likely in the study awake and following his thoughts down whatever tortured paths they lead, seeing Traveler shadows in every corner.

I leave the audience chamber for the prayer room, where Molijc and I would have breakfast and where he would conduct his morning meditations. Here I flick on a light and discover the other De Gofroy slumped, head down upon the table. Before I can turn the lights off, he raises his head and looks at me through blinking, wavering eyes.

"Aeida," he says, his voice heavily slurred. "You move about like a damn ninja."

I remain still by the doorway, watching him intently. He looks at me, his eyes unfocused and his head unsteady, and eventually he slumps back to the table. I go over to him and put a hand on his shoulder, but he does not stir. With luck, he will not remember this when he wakes tomorrow.

If not, there may be questions I, or Aeida, cannot answer. The latter is far more problematic, for if Aeida begins to wonder what is happening with his mind, he may take drastic action.

Before leaving the room, I turn the lights off and head into the corridor that leads to the Grand Regent's chambers and my old quarters. The instinct that has led me this far tells me to go to Molijc's room, where many of the secrets of the faith are kept hidden and safe—or, at least, they once were. Though it is strong, an almost nausea-inducing urge, I ignore it. There is nothing there for me any longer. Instead I go down to the end of the corridor to the room farthest from the Grand Regent's chambers, my old quarters.

The door is unlocked, and I step within and wander to the bedroom, where I turn on the lights, revealing myself lying upon the bed asleep. I do not have the same immediate reaction as I did the last time. Then I was deeply unstable, the battle with Aeida lost, though I didn't yet know it. Facing my body was the final weight that collapsed the careful walls I built to keep Aeida and that construct Aurellano out. It was too much to bear.

This time I am expecting to see myself, but the sight of me, the peaceful calm on my sleeping face, leaves me trembling violently. I have to bite my lip to stop myself from crying out. How long I stand there watching myself sleep, I cannot say. Time seems different, bending and warping, where I stand. My own thoughts escape me. Awareness drifts from me, and when it returns I find myself sitting on the edge of the bed stroking my cheek and my long, dark hair.

It is only when I notice the darkness changing outside the window, announcing morning's arrival, that I leave my old quarters and my old self and hurry back down the corridor, through the room past the unconscious De Gofroy, out through the audience chamber to where Morris stands unaware of my presence. I reach out and touch his face, and he blinks and looks at me incuriously.

Turning away, so he cannot see the sadness on my face, I return to my quarters. I can feel Aeida beginning to awaken within me. When he returns, I will disappear again. I do not know how I know this is so, but I do. Nor do I know when I will next emerge, if ever. Was this my only chance, and will I now return behind the wall of Aeida's consciousness, forced to be an observer and no more?

The strange compulsion, which I somehow mistook for instinct, continues to beckon me back to Molijc's room. It seems to come from outside me, not within. Is it some part of Aeida that has remained awake as he has slumbered? Or is it something else entirely? What can be left to discover in those quarters that I do not already know? Nothing. There is only the past there, and I want to leave it behind.

As I near my door, still confused and mulling over these odd sensations and pondering what they might mean, Meredith opens hers and peers out. She looks unsurprised to see me. "Out and about early this morning, Aeida," she says. "Trouble sleeping?"

"No more than you," I say in Aeida's timbre. Or what I hope is his.

Meredith smiles, as though I have said more than I should have. I do not wait for her to say anything more, ducking into my quarters. She is a pathetic, broken thing now. But still very dangerous. Just like the rest of us. I cannot bear to return to bed beside Ana, but I do, lying there with my eyes open, waiting for Aeida to return.

14

I awaken feeling as though I have not slept, my body dragging and exhausted. Aching, even. I sit up in bed and try to force my sluggish eyes open, trying to think of why I might be so tired. Nothing comes to mind except for Ana. It has been so long and I was in a frenzy of desire and regret. Always regret in the end, though never enough to overcome my need.

I reach out for Ana, to reassure myself that she is still there. My hand finds the curve of her body, right at her hip, and I find myself growing hard. She sits up, holding the sheets over her naked form, and smiles her empty smile.

"Aeida," she says.

"Yes?" I say.

"Is it time to get up?"

I hesitate. "Yes. I have some things I need to do."

She nods, her expression serious. "Do you need me to come with you?"

I force myself to breathe. "No. No. That's fine. Just do whatever you normally do."

Ana looks confused.

"You can stay here," I say, standing up and putting on

my clothes as fast as possible. "I'll be back soon."

She nods and smiles, eager to acquiesce. I leave the room as fast as possible, pushing my confused thoughts of her from my mind as best I can. After a hurried breakfast, where I hope that Meredith will not walk in on me, I return to the Grand Regent's chambers. Just because I am committed to the Grand Regent and whatever he is planning does not mean I need to remain blind to what Osahi and his minions are doing.

The other De Gofroy is sitting upon the throne in the audience room when I enter, a crooked smile upon his face. It only deepens when he sees me.

"You again," he says. "Always coming and going."

I ignore his remark. "Where is the Grand Regent?"

He jerks his thumb over his shoulder at the door leading to the rest of the Grand Regent's rooms. "He is talking with his wife."

"Talking? She isn't there," I say, before I can stop myself.

"Oh, I know. Doesn't stop him from blabbing with her for hours. Like I said, he's fucking crazy."

I frown, feeling I should dispute the matter with him, but knowing it is a distraction. What this man thinks of the Grand Regent is immaterial.

He leans forward conspiratorially. "What do you think? Could I get the rest of these half-men to follow me? I bet I could, and then I'd be sitting on this chair and not him."

"You don't know the first thing about the faith."

"Oh, I'm sure I could pick it up here and there. Everyone seems to want this chair, though I can't figure out why. Not much of a faith left to govern. But you and Osahi and even that woman are all eying it."

"What do you mean me?" I say, stiffening with horror. What if the Grand Regent overhears us? What if he is using the other De Gofroy to sound me out and is listening right now?

"I see you skulking around in here. Don't think I don't

remember."

I blink, unsure what exactly he is referring to. "I am here to serve the Grand Regent. I am a faithful vessel."

"Sure. Sure," De Gofroy says. "That's why you're sneaking around here in the dead of the night."

I laugh. "I know where I spent the night, old man. In the arms of the woman I love. She can tell you the same. I never came in here."

"I know what I saw, boy."

"Is that so? And how much of whatever you're taking did you have last night?"

"I don't know what you're talking about," he says, though his hand strays to the inner pocket of the shabby sport coat he is always wearing.

"You're fooling no one," I say. "Is Osahi supplying you? I wouldn't get any ideas about sitting on that chair if I were you. I have a feeling your supply will dry up the moment you get any ideas that aren't Toma's."

De Gofroy glares at me, his mouth working silently. I laugh at him and pass into the back rooms to find the Grand Regent. Though it is easy to dismiss De Gofroy's sighting of me as a drug-induced hallucination, it still gives me pause. With the strange half-remembered memories that are not my own and the sense that my mind is not entirely mine either, doubt finds its way through the cracks of my confidence. I am certain that I spent the night with Ana, and I have no recollection, or even sense, of having gone wandering in the night. And yet…

The Grand Regent is in Laila's old quarters, sitting beside the bed, watching what remains of her sleeping. His expression is so sorrowful that I regret my intrusion and want to retreat to leave him alone, but it is too late for that.

"Aeida," he says, noticing me. His eyes are red, and I wonder if he has been crying. "How is Ana?"

I flinch at the mention of her name, the prize he has given me for my loyalty. It was a mistake to come here and be reminded that all of that is a lie, one I am desperate to forget and construct into something else. To no avail.

The Grand Regent recognizes my discomfort. "It is never what you hoped, is it, Aeida? For so many years I longed for a Laila who would not betray me. She is my one true desire. Now I have her, and I have nothing. The Acolytes have ensured that we will have faithful vessels for our work. It is important work. Necessary. The fate of the universe is at stake. But there have been costs. You and I, Aeida, we are the ones to bear them."

I feel a flicker of rage that I quickly dampen. *Some of us have borne more weight than others.* I force myself not to speak. He has given me Ana and could just as soon take her away. Among other things.

As if he is following my thoughts, the Grand Regent says, in an ominous voice, "Have you succeeded in reaching Laila's memories?"

"A few, Grand Regent, but only a few. None of them reveal much of anything useful, unfortunately."

His eyes narrow. "Anything might be useful, Aeida. Tell me them."

I hesitate, unsure what to say. There are memories of things he already knows or of things I have told him. But there is nothing about the Society or its agents within the faith.

"Tell me, Aeida. I will be the judge of their usefulness. I don't need to remind you that there are many things at play right now, and much at stake. Our time may be very short."

How short? I want to ask, as well as to wonder what the Grand Regent thinks might be happening. Instead, I nod. "Of course, Grand Regent. There is one thing. She has tried to hide it from me, I think, but I may be able to discover it anyway. De Gofroy's old files that she hid away."

The Grand Regent is unable to hide his interest in the files. His eyes gleam and he stands up from the bed to come nearer to me. "Where do you think they are, Aeida?

What universe did she hide them in?"

"They're here. They're here."

"Nonsense. Utter nonsense. She would never leave them here where we could find them."

"She did," I say.

His wrath is immediate. "Don't think you can trifle with me, Aeida. I have given you everything and I can take it all away. I am no fool, and Laila wasn't either."

I take a step back in the face of his anger, but I do not back down. "I know. But in one of the memories I've come across from one of the times when she resurfaced in my world, she is thinking about how she needs to retrieve the hard drive when she returns here to face you."

The Grand Regent studies me carefully, trying to glean whether I am being truthful. "Impossible. We searched everywhere. Every nook and cranny."

"I don't know where, but I know it is here somewhere. And now that I do, I'll find it."

"See that you do," he says, his voice rasping with emotion. "See that you do."

I nod, and he returns to the bedside, looking lovingly down upon the sleeping form of Laila. He puts a hand upon her cheek and closes his eyes. The sight of it is so disturbing to me that I turn and flee the room without another word. As I go, I hear the chilling words of the Grand Regent to the wife he exiled into me.

"I will find your secrets. You should have known, after all that we've been through, that you could not defy me. But do not worry—soon the price will be paid in full."

15

I awake to rage. My whole body is suffused with it, the muscles in my legs and arms cramped from being clenched and ready to lash out for so long. Molijc's words to my dead self still ring in my ears. Even that scum Aeida, who pities himself while raping Ana every night, was disturbed by what he said.

Soon the price will be paid in full.

I will see that Molijc pays for all he has wrought. The destruction of the faith and the faithful. There will be nothing left of the Church when I am through.

All my thoughts of leaving here, leaving the Church to its fate and finding my own, are gone. They were utter fantasy. I cannot do that now. Ana and Morris deserve better. Molijc will pay. Meredith will pay. Aeida will pay. Osahi as well. Suon. They are all here and they are all unsuspecting. I will see them all bleed.

After I manage to calm myself somewhat, I dress and slip out of the room. It is the dead of the night again. That is when I awaken, it appears, when Aeida's sleep is at its deepest. The rest of the time I can lurk where he cannot see me, aware but unable to act. It is different than it was before when I returned from the void, and I do not know why. Something in us has changed. An Acolyte would be able to tell me, and that is where I head, though I cannot dare to ask him to look within me.

As I descend the stairs, I am overcome again by the compulsion to return to the Grand Regent's rooms. I ignore it, as best I can. The urge is nearly irresistible, a thought itching and itching at the back of my mind. It reminds me of the days before I joined the faith, when I was directionless and my time and energy was occupied by finding reasons why I should get high.

To distract myself from those insidious whispers, I try to formulate a plan. I cannot be forever skulking around in the night while Aeida is asleep. Eventually I will slip up, and he, or someone else, will become aware of my return. That, or I will reach the limits of what a body and mind can sustain while never sleeping. Though this vessel is evidence of just how much a body can withstand, I have no urge to further test its thresholds. What I need is to be in control, to be able to force Aeida to sleep, so that I can act when I need to.

And to stop him from touching Ana again. That is paramount.

Most important is that he not be aware, for he might tell Molijc or Meredith about my return. As much as he fears submitting himself to the Acolytes' ministrations again—and there I cannot blame him—he fears my return more. He needs to think he remains in control, even as he doesn't. The strangeness of my return, which has taken place outside of both our controls, has masked things for the moment. But for how long?

When I arrive at the second floor, emerging from the stairwell, all is quiet. There are only a few lights on and a few of Osahi's people on watch at the corridors and windows. Everyone else appears to be in bed in one of the side rooms, or else absent, which makes sense, given the hour. The guards give me a glance, but make no move to stop me. They do not consider Aeida a threat, and why would they? He is one man, and loyal to the Grand Regent they are allied with for the moment. The Watchers who stand guard around the perimeter of the campus are the real threat, and Osahi's people know it.

I return the guards' indifference and head over to the corner where De Vroes has set up his equipment. The tools of the Acolyte trade. The Orb is not visible, which is a relief in some ways, but I recognize much else of what he has assembled there. I begin to dig through one of the shelves he has set up. It is lined with bottles of various drugs: suppressants, paralytics, and compounds that can remove their effects.

I am looking for one in particular that I think may help me in my present situation, if I can remember what Morris taught me in those harried days before Molijc transferred me from my body to this false one. Then we were preparing my mind to resist the tamp, to make it more unstable than it already was, so that I might be able to engineer a return. Meredith had told me he intended to hide me in Aeida, but not about the Aurellano construct. That complicated matters considerably and made it easier for her to control me and return me to that blank slate.

Now I just need a dampener, something that will mute Aeida's consciousness and allow me to gain control. At least, in theory, if Morris was to be believed. Of that, I am no longer certain, as with so many other things. The risk, of course, is that I will inadvertently dampen my own consciousness as well, perhaps leading to a return of Aurellano, whatever that construct was.

The key is to get Aeida to take the drug while he is in control of his body, and I have some ideas on how to manage that. If I am lucky, the dampener will rid me of Aeida and this compulsion, which continues to whisper at the edges of my thoughts. Once I catch myself halting my search and looking up at the ceiling, as though I might peer through all the floors of the tower and see to the heart of Molijc's quarters. It is only for an instant, but I look at the guards to see if any of them have been watching me and seen what just occurred.

None of them are paying me any mind. It is almost as if they have been told to ignore me entirely, regardless of what I do. I push that paranoid thought aside and turn back to the shelf to find the dampener, my hands shaking a little, which is worrisome for a whole host of reasons. There is a great risk that taking the dampener will only serve to deepen the already perilous equilibrium that exists in my mind, with no guarantee that I will emerge on the other side whole and unscathed.

It is a risk I am willing to take, though. I have waited long enough for the opportunity to return here to the Church and do battle with Molijc, and the dampener feels like my only chance to ensure that happens. My time feels so short. Everything seems so unsettled, with Osahi plotting and Molijc certainly not as oblivious and out of touch as he appears. Lasinha is somewhere, I feel certain, and he will not stand idly by and let the Church he has helped build be torn apart. And who knows what the Seeker and the Society will do when they find out their supposed agent is here at the heart of the Church?

I have just located the dampener and am about to take it from the shelf when a familiar voice interrupts me.

"What are you up to?" It is Suon.

The rage that I awoke with returns in force, and it is all I can do not to whirl and attack her. My muscles quiver and I clench my jaw until it aches as I turn around.

"Get away from there," she says when I don't respond.

I don't move, still not trusting myself to speak. *You are the reason Aeida rules this body and not me. You are the reason he has Ana again. Your betrayal.*

"What's the matter with you, Aeida?" she says, concern softening her expression. "You don't look well."

You told me you loved me and then betrayed me. It hurts more than I want to admit, though I did not share her feelings. I guarded myself against her as best I could, but not enough in the end. There were feelings of a sort, and I allowed myself to believe in her, in what she said. She wore me down just enough to be able to take advantage and stick the knife in my ribs. Seeing her standing here before me now, defeated and hopeless as I am, just twists the blade deeper.

"I'm fine, Suon," I say, just remembering to use Aeida's tone.

She seems taken aback, whether because of the acid in my voice or my expression, I don't know.

"Good," she says, suddenly guarded. "You still shouldn't be here, Aeida. This is De Vroes' stuff. Go back to bed."

"What are you still doing here?" I snarl at her, unable to resist. "You told her you wanted to run away from all this."

Suon goes very still, glancing around the darkened space. No one is near, and the guards continue their scrupulous avoidance of looking in our direction. "She didn't want to, so I stayed. I...wasn't sure what to do. Maybe it's a mistake."

"Osahi always has uses for people like you."

"Does he? I don't know. He only has eyes for one thing now, and he'll do anything to get there."

"That's always been true," I say, my voice wavering dangerously.

"Probably," she says, sounding very sad. "Maybe I just see it now."

"You can always run still," I say.

"Yes," she says, looking at me carefully. "So can you."

"I'll never run. I am a faithful vessel."

"So it seems," she says. "Until someone says you aren't. Anyway, that is neither here nor there. You shouldn't be here. Osahi will get suspicious eventually. Go to bed."

I consider talking with her further, forcing her to admit that she betrayed me and to explain why. There is no point to that, though. She did, and all that matters now is that she pay for what she has done. Still I am reluctant to leave just yet. It feels like a surrender somehow. What makes me go in the end is her expression, which disturbs me. There is too much understanding there.

As I retreat to the stairwell, I glance back to see Suon watching me, as she lingers by the Acolytes' equipment, checking to see what I might have done. That she is looking there and not the shelf is a relief. The bottle of dampener is in my pocket after I slipped it there while we were talking, apparently without her noticing. Somehow I will have to find a way to return it to the shelf—after I've transferred the liquid to another vessel—before De Vroes notices it is gone. That is a problem for another night, though.

I stop on the eleventh floor and find a plastic container, for salad dressing or something like that, in the kitchenette to pour the dampener in. It is a clear liquid with a faint medicinal scent, but otherwise innocuous. If anyone, aside from Aeida, comes across it, the container should not raise too many questions, or at least not the right ones. And if I am lucky, Aeida will not be coming back anymore.

As I return upstairs to my room, I make sure to read the dosage information on the side of the bottle, before stuffing the empty bottle in the inner pocket of Aeida's jacket. Two drops dissolved in a glass of water should be enough, I decide. If that doesn't work, the dosage can be raised significantly before I run into any issues of debilitating side effects or life-threatening reactions. I am not an Acolyte, though, so this is all guesswork.

A dangerous way to live, but I don't see any other choice. There can be no coexistence, no equilibrium in this body. And there is too much at stake to leave things to chance.

Meredith is not in the hallway waiting to confront me when I return to my quarters, which is a relief. She may be watching me, though I am less concerned about that than

Aeida. From what I have seen of her, she is as indifferent to him as everyone else is. Only he cannot see it. She looks utterly lost, unable to leave the Church and unwilling to do anything to either oppose Molijc or stem the downward spiral he is on, and hating herself for that inability. Much like Aeida himself.

Ana is still asleep, and I wake her, shuddering a little as my hand touches her shoulder.

"Aeida," she says, the same half-smile on her face.

"Ana, I have something I need you to do."

She nods, eager to please, and it is some time before I am able to continue.

"You see this?" I say, holding up the small plastic container filled with dampener. "I need a couple of drops of this every morning in a glass of water. Just like this."

I pop the lid off and splash a little of the liquid into the half-empty glass of water Aeida left at the bedside. Ana watches me with an intensity that disturbs me.

"This is medicine. It's very important that I take it every morning when I get up. You understand?"

Ana nods gravely.

"Good. I'm going to put the medicine here." I snap the lid back on the container and put it in the first drawer of the night table. "You need to remember to put it in every day before I get up. Now, this is going to sound strange, but it's very important. You have to do it before I get up. I can't see you put the medicine in. Because I don't like the medicine and sometimes I think I don't need it. I may even tell you that. But I do. I really do. So it's your job to make sure I take it without realizing it. Every morning. Can you do that?"

Ana considers the question for a moment in a way that breaks my heart. "Yes," she says. "I will do that."

"Good. I'm glad. Now, it's still early, so we can go back to sleep. When I wake up, I want you to make sure I drink the water. It'll be like a test. Right?"

Ana nods. "Yes. I will make sure."

We both return to bed, Ana quickly drifting off to sleep, while I remain awake, my mind filled with thoughts it cannot contain. It is essential that I fall asleep in order for Aeida to return and Ana to apply the dampener, but that very necessity makes it impossible for me. I feel hot, as though my brain is a processor trying to compute too many functions, overheating all my components. I am trying too hard to not think, to relax and let go, even as each minute that passes feels more perilous.

What will happen if I am still awake—still me—when Ana arises? She will not be put aside, and I will do to myself what I intend for Aeida. The fear, unspoken even in my thoughts, is that I will do so anyway, regardless of who is in command of this body. I have only Morris' word on the Acolytes' drugs, their uses, and their efficacy. The consequences of what I am attempting are unknown to me. Likely they are unknown to the Acolytes, not that that would stop them. It is an easier thing to do when it is not your own state of mind that will be at risk, I suspect.

The overriding urge to return to Molijc's quarters and discover what I know is there is little help. I consider answering its call, if only in the hope that it will silence at least that part of my mind. But I know how that kind of need works—it is never quiet for long. It returns, as persistent as any predator stalking its prey.

That thought leads to another that I have managed to ignore for most of the night. Where is the Seeker? He knows where I am. At least, it is within his power to know, should he care. The Black Robes will know as well, given all the crossings I have undergone. So long as I know, nothing has been done to obscure their traces. Why haven't they moved against me, or indeed the whole Church? This would seem the opportunity they have been waiting for. The Grand Regent is harboring a known fugitive, along with dozens of others the Travelers could prove have broken the sanctions against travel between the universes. To say nothing of what the Acolytes have done to their agents Morris and Ana.

It is strange, I think, as I stare at Ana's still form in the darkness, that the Travelers never searched for her when she disappeared. Or that the Seeker never came for Morris after the Order took him. He was his agent, after all. And what of our supposed alliance? He has made no attempt to contact me, or Aeida, even though we are exactly where he wanted us.

Strange indeed, and I have no explanation for it. There will be stranger days ahead, I suspect. That is my final thought before I drift off to sleep.

16

My eyes cannot seem to open, thick with grit and heavy with sleep. My whole body feels as though it has been tied down with anchors and dropped into a sea. I am sinking slowly, the sluggish undertow dragging me ever farther into an abyss of darkness. That is what I see when I close my eyes—the void, pulling me ever closer with the force of some awful gravity that I cannot escape. The terror I feel at that makes me sit up, which only disorients me more.

Movement is overwhelming, leaving me dizzy and worried that I might vomit all over the sheets. My mouth is dry and chalky, with a strange aftertaste still in the back of my throat. There is a glass of water at my bedside, and I drain it hungrily, gasping for air. As my disorientation slowly subsides, a headache takes its place, straining at my temples, pulsing with my heartbeat.

"Son of a bitch," I say, groaning.

I reach behind me to find Ana's comforting form, but she is not there. That worries me enough to get me to my feet, and I stumble about my quarters to see if I can find her, even poking my head out into the hallway. But she is gone.

The thought chills me. Has the Grand Regent withdrawn his gift? Is he angry with me? Or has Ana gone rogue, her tamp malfunctioning? They need to be checked regularly. There are no Acolytes here to do so, except for that rogue De Vroes, so I don't know what we are supposed to do in the event she needs to see one.

I wonder if I should go talk to someone—but who? There is no one to trust. No one to confide in, and no one who would do anything. I am on my own.

My headache is now blinding me. There is a sharp point of light directly at my pupils. Behind it lies the void. There is no returning from that place. Fear eats at me, over the approaching prison of the void, my confused and stagnant thoughts, and the mystery of Ana's absence. All of them are too much to deal with in my current state, let alone attempting to leave my quarters and go about my day.

I go back to bed and lie there, hoping sleep will somehow come and that I will emerge from it whole and complete.

As soon as I entered my quarters, I could sense that I was not alone. I paused in the threshold, letting the light from the corridor spill within, and could just make out Lasinha sitting on a chair in my living room. He was not looking at me, but instead at the desk where I had a laptop. As I looked closer, wondering what could be drawing his attention, I saw that he was staring underneath the desk at the floor where the router was. And the dead man's switch, whose light had not blinked in nearly a year.

"Your router is down," Lasinha said, glancing up at me, the same false smile as always upon his face.

"Just needs to be rebooted, I imagine," I said, stepping across the threshold and closing the door.

"Indeed," he said, with a small chuckle, as though we had shared a joke.

For some reason, that made me shudder. It was not

enough that he was here in my room—though I had no illusions about my privacy here, he had to act like we were still friends. How long ago had that been?

"What do you want?" I said, going to kitchenette to get myself a glass of water.

He waited until I returned before replying. "What are you doing in the other universe?"

You know very fucking well what I'm doing. "Trying to find out what happened to Ana."

He made a face, an exasperated sound escaping his lips. "How many times do I have to tell you, she went back to the Society. What other explanation is there?"

"I can think of a couple," I said, but did not elaborate, and looked at him pointedly.

The easy smile slipped back into place, his guard restored. "That doesn't make them true."

"I don't know everything that you're doing in that little mansion of yours in the other universe. Or what you've got that kid following you around like a love-struck puppy doing, but I can hazard a few guesses."

"We are doing what the Grand Regent asks of us. For the faith."

"There was a time when you would call him by his name."

Lasinha shrugged. "He is the Grand Regent." As if that were the only explanation required.

I resisted another shudder, wondering if he had been made into one of those things by the Order as well. It would explain his odd compliance. But no. Lasinha was many things, but he was far too careful to allow anyone, even Molijc, to move against him. If that day ever came, he would vanish, like Osahi. They were both phantoms.

"I've seen what you do to people in his name." I still had made no move to sit down, and he continued to sit upon my chair, looking from me to the switch under the table from time to time, as if to remind me that he knew. He knew, and the Order could take me whenever it

117

wanted. The justification was there, and only Molijc could protect me. And that was no protection at all.

"The Acolytes' procedures are perfectly safe. No one is harmed."

"You and I have different definitions of harm."

Lasinha held out his hands. "Maybe so. But I take them at their word. They and the Grand Regent have been working on this for a long time. To make our vessels more faithful. It is a worthy goal, I think."

"With such a glowing endorsement, I'm surprised you haven't volunteered for the procedure yourself. What about your little boy, has he?"

Lasinha smiled, but I could sense his unease. Somewhere I had hit a nerve, or perhaps even he could not stomach his bullshit. "I am a faithful vessel."

I snorted. "Sure. Obedience is not the same thing as faith. I would have thought De Gofroy had taught you better."

He did not reply, picking at a piece of lint on his pants.

"What are you doing here?" I said.

Lasinha's fascination with the lint on his pants continued, until at last he looked up and met my eyes. "Osahi has gone to ground."

"Why would he do that?" I said mockingly. It was what I should have done with my people as soon as we realized the Order was watching us. Instead, I remained, exposed and precarious, uncertain why the dangling sword hadn't plunged, wondering if there was some way we could pull off our revolt.

Lasinha ignored my question. "He's taken two other High Regents with him. We've kept things as quiet as we can for now, but there will be questions that we don't have answers for soon."

"I'm sure the people asking those questions will receive a visit from your Watchers soon enough."

Lasinha flinched, though his smile remained in place. "Only if it is necessary."

"It seems to becoming more and more of a necessity. The halls will be empty around here."

Lasinha hesitated, seeming to choose his words even more carefully than normal. "Perhaps these very halls," he said, gesturing about my quarters.

I gave a small shrug, acknowledging what we both knew, that things were in motion. Better to let him believe I might go to ground than that I was planning an assault against him and the Grand Regent. Though it was possible he was aware of both things. Everything depended on Meredith, and as much as I wanted to, I could no longer trust her.

"I'm sure you recall the last time Osahi went away."

I nodded, crossing my arms, indicating my patience was wearing thin.

"There was a lot going on those days. Things were misplaced."

I smiled and declared in a loud voice. "All De Gofroy's files are in the Grand Regent's possession."

Lasinha frowned. "Good. Good. I'm glad to hear it. With everything else that has happened, all that we have achieved, I forgot to follow up on that. But it is good that you returned them all to the Grand Regent's study."

"I did," I said.

"I will let the Grand Regent know. He has been insistent on locating them. He thinks they will shed some light on what other agents the Travelers have inserted in the Church."

"I am at his service should he wish to discuss the matter," I said. "I am a faithful vessel."

Lasinha did not reply, standing abruptly and walking past me out of the room, leaving me alone with my thoughts.

Light streams in through the tall windows beside my bed, while darkness looms in my thoughts. I blink it away as I slowly return to consciousness. My body seems drawn to the bed, dragged there by some shift in gravity that has my blood trying to leave its vessels, sinking deeper within whatever lies inside. The sensation is distinct and distinctly unpleasant.

What have I done?

My mouth feels dry and chalky, coated with some foreign substance. There is a glass of water by my bed, but I know better than to drink from it, and force myself to get up and go to the bathroom to drink from the tap. The haunted and exhausted face that greets me in the mirror is not my own, and it unsettles me all over again. I splash some water on my face and try to steady my legs, which are trembling as I lean against the sink counter.

"Ana," I call out in a faint voice. There is no response.

I can't remember anything from the moment I lay down to try to sleep. There is only darkness and this moment now. I have no sense of how much time has passed. It may have been days or only hours. Whether I was awake or asleep for all this time, or if Aeida has awoken and done something, I do not know. Only Ana can say for sure, and she is gone.

What if Molijc took her away from Aeida in a fit of pique? What will I do then? My whole plan relies on her being here to provide Aeida with medicine and to keep me apprised of what happens.

The thought makes me choke in fear, and I return from the bathroom to the bed and lie upon it, hoping that these side effects, or whatever they are, pass. They do not feel like side effects. It is like a seismic shift in the delicate balance within this crowded mind has taken place.

Before, when I emerged while Aeida slumbered, I felt entirely in command. And in those moments when he was awake, I could do nothing. I was forced to watch as he raped Ana, felt the same pleasure he felt. Thrilled at it as he did. This feels materially different. If he were to emerge from the void, I do not know if I could fend him off. Instead of destabilizing him, as I intended, it seems I have managed to destabilize everything. What will emerge from this new rubble?

As I ponder that with horror, there is a knock at the door. Struggling to keep myself upright and steady, I go to open it and am faced with Meredith.

"You look terrible, Aeida," she says, her assured demeanor hiding turmoil beneath its placid surface. I know her too well.

I grunt something unintelligible and return to collapse upon the bed, not even bothering to see if she will follow. Meredith does, closing the door quietly behind her and coming to hover over me.

"Where is Ana?" she says, as though just remembering she should be here.

"I don't know," I rasp in what I hope sounds like a mournful tone. I should be sending her away, demanding she leave immediately, although that will only raise her suspicions. She can always smell me out. I should be doing anything I can to avoid her, but I have neither the strength nor the sense to do so right now.

Meredith looks at me closely, her eyes narrowing. "Odd. I'd think you'd keep a close eye on her."

I shrug and don't reply, hoping that lying down will somehow clear the murk from my head. Meredith splits and fractures before me, multiplying and then merging back into herself, as I blink at her. She puts a hand on her hip, a stance I remember so well, and I am overcome by desire and memory. Following hard upon it is fear. I cannot trust myself with her, especially not now.

"The Grand Regent sent me to see if you've discovered anything in Laila's memories. He wants to know where the files are. I really wish you hadn't brought them up. He won't shut up about them now."

I close my eyes to stop the spinning in my head and breathe out slowly. "You probably know where the files are, Meredith. Didn't Laila trust you? She must have trusted someone to take care of them."

"She only ever trusted herself. No matter what she might have believed."

I risk opening my eyes to see the expression on Meredith's face. It is fuzzy and distorted by the light, as though she has become transparent somehow. I want to ask her to close the blinds, but I don't want to raise her suspicion any more than I already have. She will begin to think that I am returning, and I cannot have that.

"So that's a no," I say.

Meredith looks down at me, as though remembering I am here. "You shouldn't have mentioned the files. If Lasinha couldn't find them after all he did, they're gone. Probably destroyed."

I cough and clear my throat, suddenly feeling very thirsty again. There is a glass of water by the bedside...but I must not drink it. *Why?*

Meredith is still staring at me. "You look terrible, Aeida."

"I'm fine," I say, forcing myself to sit up a little higher on the bed, regretting it instantly. "Tell the Grand Regent I will update him later today on what I've discovered. Is De Gofroy still with him?"

"Of course," she says. "Where else would he go? Osahi thinks he's got Molijc distracted, but it's you who's actually done the trick. It's all he can think about. Do you really have anything to update him on?"

"That's for the Grand Regent's ears only."

"No, then."

"If he wants the files, he can remove her from this body," I say with a sudden fierceness.

Meredith laughs. "You really think that's ever going to happen? Don't be a fool, Aeida—you are a vessel, nothing more."

"I have been faithful," I say.

"That's your mistake. He thinks he wants loyalty, but what he really wants is the Church he sees in his mind. He'll always be trying to get there. And she is a part of it."

"I guess I could say the same of you. Otherwise you should have left here a long time ago."

"I guess so," Meredith says in a distant voice.

The light seems to grow to a piercing point aimed at the center of my brain, where it will gouge open the void and reveal all that lies within. But what remains there now?

"What are you waiting for?" I say. "It will never be like it was."

"No," Meredith says. I can feel her looking at me.

"Then why stay?" It is a question I keep asking myself and a mistake I keep making. I should have gone, even if it meant abandoning Ana. All I have done here is hurt myself and others, and that is all my staying will do as well.

"To try to set things right."

My eyes find hers, unsteady as they are, and I feel hope, as dangerous as that is.

17

A hand on my shoulder, gentle at first and then hard, brings me back to consciousness. I look up into Ana's gorgeous eyes. They hang apart from the rest of her face, suspended in midair somewhere above her head. I smile, despite my sense of horror. It is good to see her and know she is well.

"Aeida," she says. "You need to drink some water."

I glance over at the night table where the glass is, the movement causing my head to spin and my vision to blur. It takes me some time to regain my equilibrium and for my thoughts to cohere. I look at the glass and hesitate. My mouth is so dry, but there is a taste. Metallic. There is something about the water, I'm sure, though I don't remember. The memory is there, but it is not, just like myself.

Ana looks from me to the glass. "Aeida, you need to drink some water."

She picks up the glass, and I raise a hand to forestall her. I open my mouth to say something, but only a pitiful croak emerges.

"Don't worry," Ana says. "You just need some water and you'll feel better."

She sits on the edge of the bed and lifts me into a semblance of a seating position. I try to resist her, but I am too feeble to do anything. The water. She raises the glass, and I open my mouth, realizing the futility of it. The taste is there as it splashes into my mouth, but I guzzle the entire glass, which does not even begin to slake my thirst.

Ana nods her approval. "That's good, Aeida. Do you want more?"

I nod, and she brings me another glass and helps me drink it. The taste is not there this time. Or maybe it is. I can no longer tell. She eases me back down onto the pillow.

"You're too good to me," I murmur, my eyes already falling closed. "I don't deserve this."

"Yes." Ana nods, as though what I have said is obvious.

The Watchers burst through the door without warning. By the time I was fully awake and aware, they had surrounded me, pulse weapons ready to fire. I looked warily from face to face, all of them masked by goggles and other apparatus, unable to determine who was in charge.

"What the hell do you think you're doing?" I said, trying to keep the fear from my voice.

There was no response from any of those surrounding me, no motion to even indicate that they had heard me. They remained poised and ready for a signal from someone or somewhere.

"Do you know who I am?" I said, though of course they did. "The Grand Regent will have something to say about this."

"He will indeed," the Grand Regent said, striding into the room. He waved at the gathered Watchers as though to dismiss or put them at their ease. None of them moved, alert and intent upon me. Molijc appeared not to notice, going to sit on the edge of the bed, very near to me. He smiled. "The more pertinent thing is what *you* have to say."

I glanced at the Watchers, as though gauging my chances of escape, but really stalling for time. What did the Grand Regent know? *Everything.* That seemed the safest explanation. There was no use in denying or pleading my innocence; my fate had already been determined. I had been with the Church long enough to know that, had meted out enough justice of my own to know that nothing I said now could possibly save me.

"I have always been true to the faith," I said, my face going hot with anger and shame.

The Grand Regent studied me, waiting to see if I would say more. He seemed disappointed when I did not.

"I don't need to tell you how disappointed I am. I put my trust in you… I cannot believe it has come to this. The Church needs faithful vessels if we are to achieve what De Gofroy saw was possible for us. The fate of the universes is in our hands. It is not something to put at risk over trivialities and pettiness. And yet you have. And now we are here."

"Do what you have to do," I said, affecting a nonchalance I did not feel.

He looked at me, sadness evident on his face. Was it real?

"Very well," he said, and stood. With a nod to the Watchers, he left the room.

All my memories and thoughts seem to drift just from my grasp, as though I am afloat on a sea and the current takes me just within grasp of a lifeline only to pull me away before I can seize it. The last days—how many of them, I do not know—have left me adrift and unmoored from even myself.

I feel better than I have in a long time, though I am still unsteady as I get to my feet and go to the bathroom. The mirror shows an unshaven face with sunken, exhausted eyes and a blank expression. It seems both familiar and unfamiliar at the same time. I feel separate from myself, distant and apart, as though I am another planet orbiting the sun, watching its circumnavigation from afar.

There is a foul taste in my mouth from too much sleep and medicine, though I can't remember taking anything. Ana had me drink the water, I recall, and now she is gone again. A tremor of fear seizes my heart, and I hurry back to the night table. The glass is there and it is empty. Did I just drink it, or was that some other memory from some other time?

I push those questions aside. There is too much else to attend to. Meredith told me the Grand Regent was asking questions about my progress in unlocking Laila's memories, and, as far as I know, I have not been to see him. He will be wondering what has happened to me, and what is going on. I cannot afford those kinds of questions now. They are the sort that will lead to the Acolytes being summoned to inspect me.

I amazed he has not already, given the state I was in when we had our first confrontation. The distraction provided by Osahi saved me, as did his apparent trust in Meredith to observe me and report to him. An insane trust, but he is mad, lost in his own constructions of the universe, failing to see what is right before him.

There is another possibility, of course, one that is utterly chilling. He did send for the Acolytes and they did some work on me. I would not necessarily remember. These last days, my utter confusion—and what can only be a severe reaction to some kind of drug—suggests as much. Maybe he has grown impatient with my apparent lack of progress and wants to hurry the matter on. Or perhaps my delicate equilibrium is collapsing again, without any hand to touch it.

I cannot go see him now, not in this state. He will smell my weakness, my instability. He has always had a scent for that. But I can't put him off any longer, either. I have to tell him something. My lie about the files has backfired.

Instead of putting him off while keeping him thinking that things might be progressing, it has put me at the forefront of his mind. That is a dangerous place to be.

There is also something else, which I cannot explain. Though I am loath to go and face the Grand Regent now, I feel compelled—deeply compelled—to go to his quarters. Not to see him. But to be there, to find—what? I do not know.

As I brush my teeth, I contemplate the choices that lie before me. I can continue to lie to the Grand Regent in the hopes that he will somehow give me what I want. Meredith is right, though—he will never do that. He created me. This malformed thing is what he wants, and he will never unmake it. I have given myself utterly to the faith and to him, but I will not be given any ultimate reward. I will only be asked to keep on giving until nothing remains.

We are vessels, to be used and discarded. Well, no more. But what can I do?

Go. I asked Meredith why she did not, and I should ask myself the same question. There is nothing here for me at all. I should find Ana and leave, go somewhere and spend what time remains to us before our Acolyte-marred brains make that impossible. It would not be a good life, but it would be something.

It is not what I will do, though. I cannot. I have to go to the Grand Regent's quarters and find what is there.

He is waiting for me in the audience chamber, sitting upon his throne and looking distracted, tapping a finger against his teeth. When I enter, ushered in by Morris, he glances up and smiles.

"At last, Aeida. I was getting worried."

I attempt a smile. "I apologize, Grand Regent. It has been a struggle wrestling with myself. I tried to come earlier, but I was simply too tired."

"But you have found something," he says, leaning

forward.

I swallow. "I'm getting close. Very close. But not yet. Soon, though."

The Grand Regent frowns, his disappointment obvious. Before he can say anything, I begin to talk hurriedly. "It's very difficult. She does not want to give up her secrets. At all. Every time I go into her memories, I risk bringing her back."

"Perhaps she would be more useful to me than you, Aeida. I am beginning to wonder."

"She will never tell you where they are," I say. "If the Acolytes couldn't get the answer from her, they won't be able to now."

The Grand Regent's frown deepens, but he knows I am correct. "She told them it was here. Lasinha looked, of course...perhaps that was my mistake."

I want to inquire further about Lasinha, to find out what has happened to him, but I don't dare risk enraging the Grand Regent.

"I will find it. The answer is hidden somewhere there."

"She was too well prepared by the time the Acolytes got to her," the Grand Regent says, musing in a far-off voice. "We found little of use. I suspect what we did find was planted somehow. Intended to lead us astray. And it did. I never truly understood the insidious nature of her ties to the Society and the Seekers. I always thought it was Ana alone, but clearly that was not the case. Not the case at all. They poisoned her against me."

My mind drifts from what he is saying to what lies in the rooms behind the throne room. There are secrets there. My secrets. I have to find them. It is all I can do not to think about them.

"Are you all right, Aeida?" the Grand Regent says. He is staring at me, and I am suddenly aware that he has been quiet for some time.

No, I want to say, but that would be foolish. I am saved, however, from saying anything by the arrival of the other De Gofroy. He looks at me through narrowed eyes before turning to beam at the Grand Regent, who studies him coldly.

"Is there something wrong, Grand Regent?" De Gofroy says, fidgeting a little. He still smiles, but behind it I can see the itch of need beginning to build. His eyes are dim, drained of color, and behind his forced cheer lies an exhaustion that seems as though it might match my own. He feels things slipping away, out of his control, I realize. As do I.

The Grand Regent ignores him, his eyes still upon me. "You may go, Aeida. Rest now. But I shall expect real results tomorrow. My patience is growing thin. It seems to be my fate to find myself surrounded by incompetence and betrayal. I cannot afford to wait any longer to cast the poison of the Society from the faith. If you are unable to find Laila's memories, I shall have to look to other methods."

The color has gone from De Gofroy's face, as I'm sure it has from mine. I feel my whole body trembling, but I manage to look up and meet the Grand Regent's eyes with a steady gaze. "I will not fail you," I say, though my voice sounds filled with doubt.

"See that you don't, Aeida. I am putting my faith in you."

I leave the audience chamber, the weight of doom weighing upon my shoulders. There is no way I can reach Laila, no means by which I can recover the files. If the Acolytes were unable to penetrate her defenses— something I have never heard of happening before, and which does not seem possible—then I have no hope. There is that which lies in those quarters, which some unknown part of my mind keeps urging me to return to. What it is, I don't know. It may even be the files. Or some trap Laila has set for me.

Morris nods at me as I pass through the door, and I resist a shudder. That is my fate if I fail the Grand Regent, as I surely will, though it can hardly be worse than my current tortured existence. I do not recall returning to my quarters or what happens next.

18

It is cold—that is the first thing I am aware of. The second is that I am not in my bed. I am hunched down, pressed against a wall, in some corner, surrounded by darkness. The dull red gleam of an exit sign and hard, cool floor— not carpeted like my own room—tell me that I am not in my quarters. My hamstrings ache from the act of crouching, leaving me to wonder how long I have been here. I rise unsteadily, leaning for support against the wall, my legs threatening to buckle beneath me and the darkness swimming around me blearily.

I swallow and find my mouth is dry, with that telltale metallic taste of the dampeners. It has all gone horribly wrong. Ana has dosed me. She has dosed Aeida. It has left me unhinged from this body, which is flailing against the currents and winds of the dampeners, uncertain which mind to give precedence to. I want to claw into my brain and pull myself out, let me float away free.

It takes me several more minutes to regain my senses enough so that I can try to ascertain where I am. My first thought is that I must be on one of the other floors in the tower, but the corridor I am in seems too poorly lit for that. It is also, as best I can judge in the darkness, too long and broad, and there are no windows nearby that I can see. So I am somewhere else on campus, but what building, I cannot tell. How I came to be here is an even more disturbing question, but I decide to leave that aside for the moment, at least until I know I am under no threat.

I begin to move along the corridor, still leaning against the wall for support. My eyes seem unable to focus, the darkness moving in odd and nausea-inducing ways, and I blink furiously to try to dissipate my sense of vertigo. All I can hear are my shallow, ragged breaths, which suggests the power is off in this building. There is a feeling of emptiness and stillness all around that provides further credence to that theory.

The corridor is very long, and at regular intervals I pass junctions with other hallways, marked by doors. These are locked, as is every other door I try along the corridor. That makes me uneasy, for when Aeida explored all the buildings on campus, he had no trouble going anywhere, even in the Acolytes' building. So where am I?

A muffled voice, speaking low, reaches me from behind one of the doors as I pass by. I pause on the other side to listen, but I cannot make out any words or who is speaking beyond the fact that it is a woman. There is no light passing under the door, and the dimness of the speaker's voice suggests that there is another past this one which she is behind.

I try the handle, but it too is locked. Fumbling in my pockets, I find a paperclip, which I pull out and begin to straighten with my shaking hands. It is far too serendipitous a discovery to be by chance. I, or Aeida, must have expected to encounter a locked door, though I can't imagine why we would have that expectation. Unless we were following someone and thought our way might be barred. Which meant that the woman on the other side of this door was most likely Suon or Meredith.

I consider both possibilities as I work at the lock with the paperclip, a difficult exercise with my recalcitrant hands and the darkness. Suon is not familiar with the campus, and would presumably not have keys to anything, although I had found her in the Protector's House in Lasinha's old office. But this is a different building, I feel certain. Meredith seems the better bet. Her room is secure—she would make certain of that—so she can't be calling anyone. Which means she is meeting someone here. But if that is the case, why can't I hear the other person?

These thoughts and questions distract me from the fact that I can no longer hear the woman's voice. I freeze, the paperclip falling from my hands to the floor. Footsteps sound upon the hard floor, very near, just on the other side of the door. Having only moments, and not knowing what else to do, I guess and flee as quickly and silently as I can down the corridor away from where I have come.

When I hear the door handle begin to turn, I stop and drop to the floor, staying very still. If I am right, and I was following whoever this is, then I can only hope she will return in the direction she came. There is a brief glimmer of light as the door opens, illuminating Meredith in the doorway. She casts a quick glance down the corridor in either direction, before turning back within.

"Nothing. I told you. Now who is getting paranoid again?" she says, in a gently mocking voice.

She glances again from one side to the other, as though to reassure herself of her initial conclusion, her arm still holding the door open. Her gaze seems to pass above me, not registering my presence, though I cannot be certain at this distance. I remain absolutely still, not even breathing, sweat running my face in spite of the cold floor I am pressed against.

Meredith turns back within to look at whoever she is with, that person apparently saying something, though I can hear nothing from my vantage point.

"Yes," she says, with a firm nod, her familiarity gone. "I will see that she stays in play for as long as possible. You want her brought to you?"

There is a pause, while the other replies, whether in the affirmative or the negative, I cannot say. "I'll see to it," Meredith says.

She lets the door go and it swings closed, returning the corridor to darkness. The quiet holds for a moment as Meredith does not stir, and I begin to wonder if she saw me before or can somehow see me now. I fight my urge to flee, forcing myself to remain pressed to the floor even as I begin to feel ridiculous, until I hear her footfalls along the hallway, moving away from me.

At last I can breathe, and I do so hungrily. My stomach is twisting with nerves and whatever remaining aftereffects I am suffering from the dampeners. I desperately need a drink, the metallic taste in my mouth growing more prominent and my throat aching. With some effort, I get to my feet and begin to follow Meredith before the sound of her footsteps disappears. In my current state, she is my best chance of finding my way out of this building before morning.

Fortunately, her footsteps are loud, echoing through the emptiness of the broad corridor. I follow behind, going as fast as I dare while still using the wall to support myself. She is walking at a clipped pace, doing nothing to hide her presence, and she quickly leaves me behind, the sound of her footfalls dissipating, leaving me to go on in silence.

Eventually I come to a point where the corridor opens up. There is a set of stairs before me, leading to a broad entryway lined with doors, made visible by the light coming in through the windows from what must be streetlights. On either side of me there are hallways that appear similar to one I just passed through. This space, obviously the main entry point for the building, should be familiar to me, as someone who spent so many years on this campus. But I recognize nothing, and there are no identifiers I can see through the dim light to give me any clue as to where I might be.

I proceed down the stairs, reasoning that Meredith

most likely passed this way on her way out of the building. Regardless of where she went, heading outside is likely my best chance to gain my bearings and find my way back to the tower. But as I start down, I am overcome by a wave of dizziness and have to sit down on the steps before I fall. As I clutch my head and struggle to regain my equilibrium, I hear footsteps behind me.

"Are you all right, Aeida?" Meredith says. Her tone is matter-of-fact, as though she is not the least bit surprised to see me.

I turn back and look up, trying to see her through my fractured gaze and the dim light. There is only a moving shadow, the outlines of a ghostly presence.

I shake my head. "No," I say, in a broken voice that betrays my fear. This is a dangerous moment. More than anyone, Meredith can see through me, and know who I truly am. She has more practice, after all. Every conversation with her is a battle, and I am ill-prepared for this one.

Meredith sits down beside me, and I can see more of her. She is there, a tangible thing. She puts a tentative hand on my shoulder. I recoil from her before I can stop myself. Though Aeida would do the same. Or would he? I am no longer sure. Disaster looms, and I want to flee before I reveal myself, but that may tell her as much anyway.

"Why did you follow me?"

I open my mouth and close it, not knowing how I came to be here and unsure of what sort of lie to tell. My instincts tell me that I must have been following her and that I should deny it, but there seems little point.

"Why not?" I say, attempting a mocking tone and coming up miserably short.

"What are you playing at here? You have to know the Grand Regent will see through your little façade eventually. Even if he doesn't, he'll want answers soon enough. He is not patient. And things are moving quickly."

"I wouldn't know," I say. *Keep it together*, I chant to

myself as another wave of dizziness assails me. *Don't let her know who you are.* Everything will be lost if I do.

"No one tells me anything," I add in an aggrieved Aeida tone. "So I have to find out however I can. I have to look after my interests."

"I thought you were a faithful vessel. Aren't your interests the Church's?"

I don't bother to respond, and Meredith laughs. She is studying me through the darkness, and I meet her gaze as best I can. What will she do if she finds out? Play with me, like a cat with a mouse, or turn me over to the Grand Regent for him to do the same? Probably one and then the other.

"Who were you meeting?" I say, trying to turn the interrogation against her. It cannot have been the Grand Regent or any of his people, I realize as I ask the question. Which means she is working with someone else.

"Like you, I am seeing to my own interests," she says. I can feel rather than see her smile. "You should know, Aeida, that you can put your trust in me."

"Why in De Gofroy's name would I trust you?"

Meredith squeezes my shoulder. This time I do not recoil. "That's for you to decide. But you have to trust someone, you know. Things will happen quickly now. Even you must realize that. And the only way to see to your own interests is to have friends who you can rely on."

I do not reply, and we sit in the silence and darkness for a long time, Meredith's hand still upon my shoulder. At length, she stands and reaches down to offer me a hand. I stare at her, hesitant, but in the end I take it, and we head down the stairs and out into the night.

19

Light streams through the window as I wake and wonder how much time has passed. What memories I have of the last days are jumbled and filled with gaps. I remember speaking with Meredith on the steps of that strange building, trying desperately not to reveal who I truly was. After that, I recall nothing specific. We left and returned here, but that I do not remember, just as the building and my journey there are lost to me.

How long ago that was I can't say, but it feels as though some time has passed. I was awake for some of it, but what happened then is gone as well. There is only a vague awareness that I was conscious at some point, but I do not know what I did.

Was Aeida in command then? If he was, why was I not aware with him? That has been the case since I returned, but now it seems we may have reversed our positions through some effect of the dampeners. Perhaps he is somewhere inside me now, watching and laughing at my foolishness. Even if that is not the case, it is clear the dampeners have affected me adversely and I cannot risk taking any more in the hopes that I can take control from Aeida.

For now, I will just have to trust that I can maintain command for enough time to get what I need done. My plans, ill-formed beyond their intent, will need to be accelerated. But what can I do? I cannot thwart Molijc's and Osahi's desires if I don't know what they are planning. This will end badly, unless I get help. But there is no one here to help me. I cannot even trust my own mind.

Ana is not in my room, and that is another question without an answer. If there is something significant in her absence, I don't know, but I cannot worry about her now. She will ultimately be wherever Molijc or the Order wish her to be. I need to make certain I do not suffer her fate if I am to be of any help to her.

My first task is to remove the dampener from my room. I cannot have Ana returning and dosing me with it any further. Given how many days I suspect have passed, I assume De Vroes has discovered the drug is missing and a search has begun. That will give me the opportunity to insert a little chaos into their ranks.

After pouring what remains back into the bottle it came in, I head below, taking the stairs, the bottle tucked into Aeida's leather jacket. I stop to grab something to eat from the kitchen on the eleventh floor. It is empty, which I am surprised to find disappoints me. I want to see Meredith again, though I cannot imagine why. She is the reason I am trapped in this body and in this hopeless situation. She cannot be trusted.

And yet I find myself thinking of her last words to me: *I want to set this right.* Despite myself, I want to believe her.

There is a half-filled pot of coffee on one of the counters, and I am sorely tempted to have a cup, even as my own recent experience makes me leery. For all I know, De Gofroy is spiking it with whatever he is on. Or perhaps Molijc is hoping to spur on Aeida's memory retrieval. In the end, I decide it is too dangerous, and drink some water from the tap and make some peanut butter and honey sandwiches from the meager supplies in the kitchen. Is there less there than there was before? I cannot remember.

I finish one and take the other with me as I descend below to see what Osahi is up to. A cacophonous symphony of construction noises greets me as I pass between the sixth and fifth floors, and I pause to listen for a moment while I finish the last of my sandwich and try to recall what was originally on those floors. Hierarchy quarters and offices, if I remember correctly. Aeida wandered through there earlier and found it abandoned, though I do not trust his recollections on the matter, or mine on his. They are confused. Everything feels incorporeal and incomplete.

The doors to both floors are locked, which piques my curiosity further. I descend to the fourth floor and try to take the elevator to either the fifth or the sixth, but someone has locked them out from the elevator. Though it would be a simple matter for me to override the elevator, or pick the lock to the doors in the stairwell, I do not, and continue my descent to the second floor. The answers to these new mysteries can be found there, I feel certain.

At first glance, as I leave the elevators and move out into the open area of the second floor, nothing seems to have changed. The guards still keep their vigil and De Vroes still has his equipment in the far corner. As I study things closer, I see that many of the other rooms that were once occupied have their doors open and appear empty. The stacks of equipment and supplies once scattered throughout are gone. Something is happening. Whatever Osahi is planning, he has put it in motion.

One of the guards is glaring at me as I contemplate all the changes, the first time one of them has taken any interest in me. I am suddenly conscious of the bottle of dampeners in my pocket, which I need to dispose of, and which would raise all sorts of questions I do not want to answer should he find it on me. To avoid that, I start forward, heading vaguely in the direction of De Vroes' work area. I can still feel the guard watching me as I go, and I feel a twinge of exasperation.

Before I can reach De Vroes' work area, Suon emerges from one of the side rooms and intercepts me. "Back again, are we? You didn't get everything you needed the first time?"

I flinch at her words, my face going hot with embarrassment and anger. "What are you talking about?"

"I saw you taking whatever it was you took from De Vroes' shelf. Drugs, I assume, to help with whatever is going on in there." She points at my head, and I flinch again. "Don't worry. I didn't tell him. Or Osahi. He hasn't noticed yet either. Or, if he has, he hasn't bothered to tell anyone."

My anger is white hot, blurring my vision. Yet again, I've allowed this woman to humiliate me and put her in a position to destroy me. How can I be such a fool? With great effort, I manage to calm myself. Now is not the moment to succumb to emotion and lose everything. My life is in the balance, if Osahi is starting his insurrection, and I need to buy myself some time.

For what? Revenge is out of the question now. Osahi will be the one to exact his vengeance, and I will be one of the people whom he looks to take his pound of flesh. The only thing now is to run. But where and to what end?

"What do you want?" I say, wondering if the flurry of thoughts is visible upon my face.

"You know what I want, Laila," she says. "Nothing's changed."

I am so stunned at her words that I cannot move. When I do it is to glance around furtively to confirm that no one else was near enough to overhear what she said. "What the fuck are you playing at?" I say, my voice shaking along with my hands.

"I'm not playing, Laila," she says. "And my offer still stands."

"Some offer," I say, gesturing around me. "Look what it got me."

"That was your choice," she says, her voice infuriatingly gentle. "I went with you, remember. I didn't know Osahi had already sold you out."

"You were the reason he knew who I really was," I say, barely able to keep my voice low.

My vision keeps coming and going, and I have to force myself to breathe. I imagine myself strangling Suon with my bare hands, and for a moment I decide that I will. There is no hope in returning myself to my body or in trying to exact some measure of vengeance against Osahi or Molijc. This may be my only chance for justice, however arbitrary. But that is no justice at all, and I know it.

"No," Suon says in a fierce whisper. "No, I never betrayed you. Osahi set you up. He knew who you were from the beginning."

"I don't believe you."

"Believe what you want," Suon says. There are tears in her eyes. "I told you I loved you, and it's the truth. You're the only reason I'm still here. I wanted to help you get back."

"Spare me this bullshit," I say, still quivering with fury, though it is slowly dimming as I wonder if what she is saying could be right. Did I actually pass the Eye when De Vroes administer, or did it just reveal who I was? Or had Osahi's Black Robe Nicola overhead Morris using my true name when we made our escape from the ferry? Both, I have to admit, are possibilities. But so is Suon. "Osahi sent you to keep an eye on me. You both played me from the first."

"He never told me who you were. I swear it. I only figured it out in Arequipa. He knew all along, though. And he did send me to keep an eye on you. Because he wanted to know what you were up to. But he didn't tell me who you really were because he doesn't trust me."

I laugh at her. "Doesn't trust you? If he doesn't trust you, then why are you still here?"

142

"Yes, why am I still here and not up on the fifth floor? Osahi's cut his deal with the Acolytes and he's about to get everything he wanted. He doesn't need the guards. The Acolytes will keep the Watchers in line. So why are they here? To keep an eye on me and De Vroes. Because he doesn't trust us."

I look around the room at the various guards and am forced to admit that she is right. They are all watching the two of us, not the various approaches.

"I don't believe you," I say again, though there is no force behind it. "You're the only one who could have told Osahi who I was."

Suon shakes her head. "No, I wasn't. And I didn't. But I'm not going to argue with you. I'm done with waiting too."

"Of course," I say. "Let me guess, you want me to go with you?"

Suon looks at me. Her expression is serious and there is hurt in her eyes. "Yes. If you want to. But I won't wait for you any longer. There's not enough time. Osahi is moving, and once he's secured his position, none of us is safe."

She doesn't wait for my reply, turning and walking stiffly away. I watch her go, my anger vanishing, leaving me feeling hollow and empty, a shell of a thing. When she has disappeared from sight, I retreat the way I came up the stairs, leaving the dampener near the doorway of the fifth floor, where the sounds of construction continue unabated.

I return to my quarters and throw myself upon the bed, alone with my thoughts and wanting to be as far from them as I possibly can. There are no safe directions and nowhere for me to go.

20

I fall asleep, and when I awaken several hours later, my thoughts are sluggish with sleep, but I feel no disorientation. There is no sense of gaps, of things missing, and no other immediate side effects. No odd and inexplicable compulsions to return to the Grand Regent's quarters. It is an immense relief. Most importantly, I am myself. Aeida is gone and I feel free. For the moment, at least, I have won, although that feels a hollow victory. Now, I have to somehow make it count.

Ana is watching me from a chair across the room, her normal vacant gaze changed a little. She appears anxious, if I were to put a word to it.

"Do you need water, Aeida?" she says.

"Not right now, thank you," I say, wincing slightly glad that I removed the bottle of dampeners.

"Are you sure? You told me to make sure you drank the water."

"Yes," I say. "You did well, Ana. I don't need the water anymore. That's why I took the bottle away. It's gone. You don't need to worry about that anymore. Thank you for your help."

Ana smiles, pleased to have been of use, and I feel an

ache in my chest. It is almost too much to bear. I get up and wash my face, trying to choke down the sobs rising within. When I have regained my control, I go back to see Ana.

"I have to go out," I say. "Will you be here when I get back?"

"Of course, Aeida," she says with a nod.

"Good," I say, wanting to scream and leave my quarters before my horror overwhelms me completely.

Outside the door, I pause and gather myself, trying to determine my next steps. There are none. If Suon is right, Osahi has forged an alliance with the Acolytes, and Molijc will soon be removed. Once Osahi has established himself as Grand Regent, I will be of no use to him. It is clear he wanted me as a bargaining chip to get him through the door, and as another potential distraction for Molijc in case the other De Gofroy proved ineffective. With that at an end, he will get rid of us, since we are both a threat. Aeida as a true believer in Molijc and Lasinha, and myself as a potential rival to his Grand Regency.

As these thoughts, and the questions they spark, overwhelm and paralyze me into inaction, Meredith steps out of the door to her quarters. She smiles at me, a knowing, mocking smile.

"All quiet on the home front, Aeida?"

"That is none of your concern," I say, brushing past her as I head for the elevators.

"Well, at least your lady has returned. Is she still dosing you? I do hope that the medicine takes. Drugs are tricky, as the Grand Regent's esteemed guest will be the first to tell you."

I stop in the middle of the corridor, staring straight ahead, refusing to turn around and look at her and the triumphant little smirk I know is on her face. Morris is standing at the doorway to the audience chamber, as always, and he looks down at us incuriously. Whatever he hears he will be able to remember and repeat to the Grand

Regent, so I will have to watch what I say to Meredith carefully. As she well knows. I also know, I realize, where Ana has been disappearing to these last few days.

"I hope you took good care of Ana," I say, turning back to Meredith and giving her a sour smile. "I would hate for any harm to come to her."

"A little late for that concern now, isn't it, Aeida."

"Perhaps, but I've been late arriving to understanding on many things, it seems."

A twitch of a smile passes Meredith's lips and disappears. "Don't be so hard on yourself. You haven't been yourself lately."

"I guess not," I say. She knows the truth as well, it would seem. How many others do? It is a disturbing thought on many levels, perhaps most importantly because no one has acted upon that knowledge yet. Am I so unimportant that I can be left to act unmolested, with Meredith and Suon, and whoever else, confident I will do nothing to thwart their plans?

Perhaps they are allowing me to keep up this pretense because they care about me. Certainly Suon would claim that, not that I believe her. Meredith would as well, and she would be telling the truth, in her way. Even if she would still use what she knows to her own ends when the opportunity best presents itself. That is what she is, and I cannot forget it, no matter what my emotions might be telling me right now.

"You are still the same," I say. "Always."

"You don't sound disappointed."

I shrug. "I'm over being disappointed in who the Grand Regent chooses to keep close to him. I am a faithful vessel, after all."

"Indeed," Meredith says, her voice weighted with irony. "As am I, if it comes to that. I've always put the needs of the faith first."

I open my mouth to dispute her claim, but fall silent recalling Morris' presence. If this becomes too personal, even Molijc, as distracted as he is at the moment, will begin to suspect something is up. Assuming Meredith hasn't already told him.

"That's what I was doing last night," she says in a low voice, looking past me at Morris.

"Is that so?" I say, thinking of her words to me on the steps. How I had a choice to make. Who would I trust? Suon has just extended a hand to me, offering a way out of this mess, however limited. Will Meredith do the same? There was something before that encounter on the steps, something I saw or heard. When I try to reach for it in my head, it is gone, a fog that dissipates when light is put to it.

"It is. I told you I wanted to set things right. And I meant it."

There is a pause, both of us hesitating to speak, and we share a charged glance that sets my heart racing. We both look away immediately, reluctant to give in to our arising feelings. This is as dangerous as whatever Osahi is planning, I tell myself halfheartedly. It is true, and I know it is, but I am no longer sure I want to believe it.

After so long running, betraying and being betrayed, and doing battle with seemingly everyone I once stood with, I want to trust someone. And, in spite of everything that has come between us, I want that person to be Meredith. I want to be done with all this, all the intrigue, all the machinations that will only lead to more people becoming hurt. If Meredith gave me Suon's offer—to walk away from all this and never look back—I would take it without hesitation. But I don't know if it is in her to do that.

"Seems like a lot of things are happening right now," I say, breaking our silence and nodding at the floor.

Meredith looks down as well, though her expression is filled with disdain. "Osahi is not half so clever as he thinks he is."

"I wouldn't underestimate him. You, of all people, should know that."

"I know exactly what Osahi is," she says. "He is more weak and vainglorious than the people he accuses of being. The Grand Regent is the one you're underestimating. I would think someone like yourself, Aeida, would know better than that. You've been at his side for so long."

I glance over my shoulder at Morris, who continues to look in our direction without apparent interest. "I would trust the Grand Regent more if he still had Lasinha here to give him counsel. I fear he has sent away his most loyal ally."

Meredith rolls her eyes at me. "I wouldn't say that in the Grand Regent's hearing. He's convinced Lasinha betrayed him, and he may be right. I don't know."

"He may be. It's just surprising to me."

"You always did love him, didn't you?" Meredith says.

I laugh, unable to help myself. "Yes. But like I said, I've been late to understanding a lot of things. I may still have some understanding to come to."

Meredith laughs as well and looks down the corridor at Morris again. "What are you doing now? Whatever you're up to, you know it won't make any difference."

"Maybe so," I say, with half a shrug. *I still have to try.*

She goes to the door to her quarters and pushes it open, beckoning with her head. "Why don't you come in for a while? I'm sure we can find better uses for your time."

Meredith does not wait for my reply, disappearing within. I stand in the hallway looking at the threshold, as though it were a perilous crossing. It is. Nothing good can come from going in there. I know this. But she is right: I need to decide who to trust. And I know what I want.

I glance back one last time at Morris, still watching me as he stands vigil. His indifference now seems to be that of a jailer observing the condemned. I turn and pass through the door to discover my fate.

Everything about this moment with Meredith is both

familiar and unfamiliar at the same time. This body, so fundamentally not my own, is one I have become accustomed to, so when Meredith leans across to kiss me, I am no longer surprised or horrified at its response and the pleasure I derive from it. I expect it.

Which is worrying in its own way. If this body is now so familiar that it feels like my own and not some foreign construct, what does that say about me? Will I ever be able to go back to my own?

It impels an urgency to my every movement with Meredith, whether out of desperation or a need to forget my predicament. Perhaps both. Any time spent with her is always more than one thing, both of us wary and circling, not entirely trusting the other, and being turned on by that uncertainty. It is the spark that lies at the center of everything between us.

Still, it surprises me how quickly we fall into old ways. This woman has betrayed me—and I her—and yet when we are together, it is as though we have not spent a day apart. That easy intimacy is disorienting. It feels wrong and so very, very right. I want to lose myself here and never come back, never return to whatever lies beyond that door. Osahi. Molijc. Let them battle to the ends of the universes with the Travelers and the Acolytes and Seekers. I want no part of it.

And yet here I am, inextricably binding myself to the one person who I suspect will never leave this madness. It is laughable, and I hate myself for it. But I cannot stop. We have sex in a frenzy, until it dies out, and then tenderly as exhaustion slowly takes hold. In the end I am left aching and raw.

The sun is gone from her window, the light slowly going from the sky, when we finally subside and lie next to each other, our hands intertwined.

"What do we do now?" I say.

Meredith sits up and traces a finger along my chest. A familiar gesture. I watch it for a time and have to close my eyes as I remember that it is not my chest. This is not my body. She seems to notice and takes her hand away.

"I don't know," she says. "I don't know what any of them are doing. Osahi will never trust me again, of course. Molijc is…"

"Divorced from reality," I say, though what I really want to tell her is that he is mad. Batshit crazy.

"Not as much as you think. Not as much as he lets on. You need to be careful around him. If he suspects you have returned…I don't know what he'll do. He's capable of anything, especially with Osahi trying to unseat him."

"We have to get out of here," I say, thinking aloud. "There's nothing here for us. Not anymore."

It is not the truth. Ana is here. Morris. Whatever remains of my body. They are all in danger if Osahi is victorious in the days to come. He will rid himself of any remnants of the Watchers' Order and their crimes the first chance he gets, even if it means condemning its sufferers to this cruel purgatory.

"There is one thing here for you," Meredith says, seeming to echo my own thinking.

"What good is it to me if there is no one to return me to that body?"

She is silent for a time, as though considering her thoughts. At length she says, "I may be able to help with that. Osahi's pet Acolyte is not the only one with questions about the path the Grand Regent is leading them down."

"And you think this Acolyte would be willing to restore me?" I say, a note of caution in my voice.

"He might," she says. "If he thinks you might help end this tyranny and set the Church on the right path."

"I see," I say. But I no longer believe. That is the truth; I feel it in the core of myself. If I am restored to my true body, free to do what I choose, able to go where I want, I will not remain here and be part of this madness. Even if that restoration is impossible, I will go. Anything to be away from this. All the lies, all the betrayal. At the core, that is all there is left of the faith and of what De Gofroy built. It may have been all there was to begin with. I am sorry to say it. I gave myself to it and it has taken everything.

"Think of Ana. Think of Morris. And all the others," Meredith says, sensing my doubt. "We can help them all. We can make this right. And we can restore the faith."

There is nothing to be restored. That is what I want to say, but I hold myself back. If I have a chance to restore all of those who have suffered because of me, then I have to take it. After all I have done, I cannot abandon them. I would never forgive myself.

"Talk to him," I say, closing my eyes. "Let's see what he has to say."

"I will. I will," Meredith says, unable to contain her excitement.

I feel only dread, but then, I have been here before. Everything with Meredith is never what it seems, and this is undoubtedly the case now. This feels like a trap. What happened before we met on the steps? My stomach twists at the thought. I have allowed myself again to be brought here, to be put in a position where I need Meredith. Maybe this time will be different, I tell myself, but it feels like a joke.

I have to trust someone, and I want to trust Meredith. She is not to be trusted. That is what she is, and this is what I am. We play each other, each trying to extract an advantage, each knowing the other is doing it. And it never ends and never will. I thought I had ended it back at the farmhouse when I said my goodbyes. That felt like forever. Instead it was weeks. Why do I still want her, after all that she has done? I don't know. Does she ask herself the same question? I want to believe that she does.

The questions continue to swirl around in my head. I cannot stop them. They leave me exhausted. Meredith is saying something. She will reach out to the Acolyte first thing in the morning. My eyes, still closed, will not open.

151

Sleep drifts in and will not release me.

I dream, although it does not feel a dream. There is none of the usual unreality or weirdness. But I am aware that I am not awake, that this is a dream that I am experiencing. Despite that, I am helpless to do anything. I cannot change what is happening and I cannot force myself to wake up, no matter how much I flail against the invisible boundaries I barely sense.

They are there and they hold me tight to this place. More a time than a place, as I see myself walking down these same corridors not so long ago. It feels as though an epoch has passed. None of the brightness now remains, none of the hope. Not that much remained even in those moments as Molijc and Lasinha slowly tightened the noose around my neck. But the Church at least was still something to believe in, still worth fighting for. No longer.

Aeida is returning, I realize with a sudden start of clarity, the dream going hazy, repeating itself. I walk down the same corridor again and again, never reaching anywhere. Though I try to resist, try to stop myself from going down the corridor again, I cannot. Sleep has a hold of me in a viselike grip and Aeida is ascendant. I cannot allow this to happen now, at this moment, when I have, yet again, made myself so vulnerable to Meredith. Watching her is paramount. I scream at myself to fight, to wake up, but nothing happens. The dream goes on, and I proceed down the corridor again, having already lost that battle.

As I do, I realize with a growing sense of horror—the terror of a nightmare—when I was walking down this corridor and who I was going to see. This cannot be happening. Not again.

Meredith met me in the corridor, coming from Molijc's quarters. We shared a wary glance, neither of us daring to speak, not knowing what kind of surveillance had been installed in these corridors. Though the hallway was well lit, it felt dark and shadowed, whether because of the lateness of the hour or my own troubled state of mind.

Exhaustion worked at the edges of my thoughts, from days spent preparing for the hours to come. Hours that I suspected would prove futile, even as I fervently hoped they would not. Everything was in place now. Morris and I had put all my people on full alert, to be ready to seize control of all the Church's main transfer channels. We had sent Lasinha on a chase after his pet Aeida and told our agents to prepare to go dark so that they could not be traced.

Molijc and Lasinha were aware of all this, at least in part. Meredith had seen to that, at my request. But they did not know when we planned to act. Meredith had told them we weren't ready, that we were still preoccupied with figuring out who, aside from Aeida, was tracking us. If it all went to plan, we would have control of the channels, stranding Lasinha and his Watchers in their universes, leaving Molijc and the Church Hierarchy here. By the time the Watchers recovered, Molijc would be deposed and I would be Grand Regent. The High Regents would be beside me as I made the announcement to the faithful over our networks.

It all depended on Meredith. If she revealed even a whisper of this to Molijc or Lasinha, they would be ready and we would be walking into a trap. Morris had warned me against using her, but I decided to for two reasons. One was that she was our best chance of misdirecting Molijc and Lasinha. They would trust her reports and believe her when she said she was acting as their agent and pretending to be mine. The fact they would have the similar doubts to my own about her trustworthiness would only help sow confusion about our own aims.

That was what I'd told Morris, and it was something I believed, more or less. The second was not something I could tell him, though certainly he guessed it, and it was the real reason why I had placed my trust in her. There was no point in being Grand Regent, in restoring the faith and the Church, if Meredith was not with me to do the work. I had been so alone after I sent her away at Molijc's request, and I swore I would not be so alone again.

All of this passed through my mind in an instant, and hers as well. I could see it in the guarded way she looked at me, reluctant almost to meet my eyes. The hour was almost upon us, and this "chance" meeting had been prearranged so that we could confirm all was well. The weight of the moment was upon us both, and we were reluctant to speak and risk giving voice to the turmoil we both felt. Or so I thought.

"All is well?" I said. An awkward phrasing to an awkward question. But all our interactions were awkward and freighted, and if anyone were watching, they would not necessarily think anything amiss.

"Yes," Meredith said, with a half nod. "And how are you?"

"The same."

"Good." A hesitation. I wondered what it meant. "I'm glad."

I nodded, ready to pass by her to make my rendezvous with Morris. Meredith didn't let me, standing in my way, her expression even more guarded. Before I realized what she was doing, she reached for me to draw me into an embrace. I hesitated, uncertain what she meant by it and what anyone observing us might think, but in the end I pulled her close and held her tight, barely able to disguise the emotion I was feeling. This was the culmination of months of sacrifice and hard work. Soon we would be together again.

"I love you," I whispered in her ear, my lips not even moving.

There was no response from her to my words. No tightening of her arms, no indication that she even heard what I said. It was then I felt it. The distance that was in her expression was not to guard against others seeing what she was thinking, but me. She was going to betray me.

As we withdrew from each other's arms, I looked into her eyes and saw the same mask Meredith always wore, nothing to say what she was really thinking. We parted ways without another word, and I went to the elevator and left the tower. I did not keep my rendezvous with Morris. He would understand what message to draw from that.

Instead I wandered the campus for what I understood would be the last time in a long time, if I ever managed to return. I looked at the buildings in the darkness in a way I rarely had before, and they felt utterly changed, nearly unrecognizable to me. Meredith's betrayal seemed to have created a tectonic shift, creating a place where I no longer felt I belonged.

At length I returned to my quarters to await my fate, preparing myself for what would come next. Morris and I had anticipated this eventuality as well, of course, even if I had never truly believed it would come to this. There was one question I could not shake and which I still have no satisfactory answer for. Had Meredith been unable to hide her betrayal from me, or had all that been deliberate, an attempt to warn me?

21

It is the need that awakens me, inexplicable and unaccountable, driving me onward. Ana lies beside me, and I long to take her into my arms, to feel her again as I have felt her. But the compulsion will not let me rest. It talks in my ear, and though I try to ignore it, I cannot. What is it that drives me to return to the Grand Regent's quarters? What lies there, waiting for me to discover it?

I sit up in bed, peering around in the darkness, letting my eyes adjust to its shadows. My hand rests on Ana's naked hip, and I squeeze it. She shifts in her sleep, responding to the pressure of my fingers, and murmurs something unintelligible. Only then do I realize that it is not Ana beside me, but Meredith. I leap from the bed, sick with horror. Laila has returned.

How the fuck did I not realize?

"No, no, no, no, no."

Meredith stirs again, and it is only then that I realize I am speaking aloud. I snap my mouth closed, hurry into my clothes, and flee her quarters before she awakens. In the corridor I stand alone, reeling like a drunkard, wondering how I have found myself in this nightmare totally unaware, and how I will get myself out.

Aside from the memories, which seemed to grow from somewhere within me, there was no sign of her. I did not feel her presence or sense her lurking behind my thoughts. She was not there, that much I feel certain. The strangeness of the past days—my exhaustion and the other symptoms of some mysterious ailment—must have been harbingers of her return. Yet I have no memory of it, no recollection of how I ended up in Meredith's bed. And though I am frantically scanning my mind, probing at the void that seems even more dangerous than ever, I can find no sign of her now.

"This is impossible," I say, catching myself at the last second.

Morris approaches, having evidently overhead me. "Is everything all right, Aeida?"

"Yes," I say, touching my head. "Just a strange dream. Shook me up a little. You should return to your post. You don't want the Grand Regent to be unguarded."

Morris looks at me for a moment before returning to the door. His empty eyes and blank expression unsettle me even more than usual. I hurry back into my quarters, not wanting anyone else to stumble upon me while I am in such a distressed state. Once I am safely inside, I collapse against the door, crumbling to the floor, unable to keep the sobs in any longer.

Laila has returned. My body is no longer my own.

I want this to end, though I do not know how. There is no one who will get Laila out of me, and if the Grand Regent were to realize she has returned…

That ominous thought leads me to another: the Grand Regent demanded answers tomorrow. But I have no idea how much time has passed since he gave that order. At some point he will send Meredith to get those answers and I will have to tell himself something. But will I be me, or will it be Laila who faces him?

In the end, the compulsion wins out; I can ignore it no longer. I leave my quarters and march down the hallway, past Morris and into the audience chamber. To my surprise, the lights are still on, and I pause there, listening to see if the Grand Regent or De Gofroy are awake and nearby. Hearing nothing, I proceed to the door leading to the Grand Regent's quarters. As I am turning the handle to the door, I hear the Grand Regent's muffled shout.

"Did you take me for a damned fool?"

I have never heard him so enraged, and I freeze where I am, certain that he sees me somehow and is talking to me. A voice is raised in response, though I cannot hear what is said. It sounds like De Gofroy, and it sounds as though he is pleading.

"Useless bastard. You thought you could pull one over on me? This is my world. I've been in this from the beginning. You are an amateur. Nothing but a grifter. It only goes to show how singular an intelligence the real De Gofroy had."

Though I long to linger and listen to the rest of what the Grand Regent has to say—how satisfying it is to hear De Gofroy getting his deserved comeuppance—I dare not. I don't want one of them to leave the study, where the voices appear to originate, and discover me listening. That would only succeed in turning the Grand Regent's wrath upon me, and I have things that need doing. Even if I am uncertain of what they are.

The compulsion takes over as I pass from the audience room deeper into the Grand Regent's quarters. I enter a kind of fugue state—aware, but unthinking, simply allowing my unconscious, or whatever this is, to lead me where it pleases. It takes me to a corridor, at the end of which is a set of quarters. From Laila's memories, I know it is the Grand Regent's.

I turn on the lights, revealing a well-appointed space, filled with more stolen Mayan treasures and antique furniture. There is a living room, with a television and computers, and a small kitchen, both of them empty. The smell of dust is heavy in the air. After a quick, covetous glance around, I proceed to the bedroom. It is also empty, to my relief. I feared Laila would be here, awaiting the return of the Grand Regent.

Here I do not even glance around; I go unerringly to the corner of the room, where a large safe is bolted into the wall. Without a thought, I open it, though I have no idea how I know the combination. *Laila does.* That sends a chill through me, but does not stay my hand, even as I want to flee. I am too close now, and whatever has driven me here will not allow me to escape.

Within I find stacks of bills in various denominations—from various universes, no doubt—along with some gold coins and diamonds. There is a fortune here, beyond my imagining, enough to start a new life anywhere. But that is not what I am here for, so I ignore it. On the lowest shelf of the safe there are papers of various sorts, some written in the Grand Regent's hand, others typed. Tucked in among them, almost hidden from view, are two secure hard drives. There is nothing to distinguish between the two, beyond the fact that they are two different brands, but I pull one out without hesitation. This is what I have come for.

I take one last lingering look at the fortune there for the taking before locking the safe again. I retrace my path through the quarters, pausing in the living room to see if one of the computers there is working. The first one I try flickers to life, and I connect the hard drive to it, to see what treasure I have stolen. There are vast numbers of folders on the drive, all with names of people attached to them. Within each one there are more folders with names and dates attached.

These are De Gofroy's files, I realize. This may even be the hard drive Laila stole from his study. A quick search proves that assumption correct. There are no folders on Laila, Lasinha, and the Grand Regent. Only their reports on others remain. I do several searches, even trying to see if any traces of the deleted files remain. Lasinha, or others, will have tried to do the same already, and I have no more luck than them.

Why does Laila—for that has to be where this compulsion is coming from—want these files again? There is nothing here that she, or anyone else, has not already seen, nothing that can be used against the Grand Regent. The missing files are what Lasinha was so desperate to find, because of what they might say about the Grand Regent.

I search again for anything that might illuminate what is going on, but nothing is revealed. My eyes begin to blur and I have to stop, exhaustion beginning to consume me. I miss Lasinha. He would have known what to do and what all this might mean. Instead I am left to face all this alone, while my own mind conspires against me without my even being aware of it.

Moving in a haze, I retrace my steps through the Grand Regent's quarters, returning to my own, the hard drive in my hands. I can feel sleep swallowing me up, its undertow pulling me steadily deeper into the darkness. Before it overwhelms me, I hide the hard drive, sliding it in the narrow space between the bed frame and the wall, pushing it back as far as I can so that it is not visible.

Ana is lying asleep on the bed, a wondrous smile on her face. I try to fight the sleep that is slowly consuming my conscious mind, to be with her, to make this moment of her bliss mine. That battle is already lost, though, and as I crawl into bed beside her, I am already slipping away.

FOUR:

A FAITH BETRAYED

22

Ana is beside me when I awake, still sleeping and as beautiful as always. I don't recall returning to my room. Worse, it feels as though I haven't slept. I know what that means. Aeida felt the same way when I returned. What was he up to while I slept? And is he still aware, watching everything, now?

That is a disturbing thought, to say the least, and it sends me from my room to Meredith's door. It now seems utterly essential that I restore myself to my body and that I do so as soon as possible. I cannot risk Aeida doing things without my being aware of them, particularly with Ana so near. The equilibrium that exists in my mind—if one does—still seems to be shifting after my experiment with the dampeners, and I can no longer assume I will be the one who remains in command of this body when it settles.

There is no answer to my knock on the door. When I try the handle, I find it is open and I go within, calling out Meredith's name. The rooms are empty, only the twisted sheets on the bed giving any evidence that she was there recently. I swallow, my heart thudding in my chest, and hurry to the corridor, where I find Morris standing vigil by the audience chamber.

"Have you seen Meredith?" I say, my breath sticking in my throat.

He nods, happy to help. "She went downstairs an hour ago."

To breakfast, expecting to find me there, no doubt. I thank Morris and hurry to the kitchen on the eleventh floor. It too is empty, and there are no signs that anyone has even been there this morning. No dirty dishes in the sink, no crumbs upon the table, no half-drunk pot of coffee. None of it appears out of the ordinary, but my instincts tell me it is.

There is something wrong, but I can't decide what. Has Meredith already betrayed me, the morning after regaining my trust? That is not her style, I tell myself as I recall last night's dream, or memory, or whatever it was that this mind held me hostage to. Meredith will wait until the moment when the betrayal will cut the deepest, when I need her help the most. It may be now and I just don't realize it.

I pause, trying to slow my panic and my breathing. She must have had something to attend to—maybe she has gone to make contact with the Acolyte, as she said she would last night. That reassures me somewhat. She would need a secure channel and a location where she could be certain the Grand Regent would not have ears. Or perhaps she is back at the building with the steps where we had our encounter the other night.

I will see that she stays in play. The words come back to me, the fog of my memory stabilizing. Was she talking about me? I can hear her voice coolly explaining all of this, how it is all part of what she has to do to keep Molijc, or whoever it was she was meeting, secure in her trustworthiness. It will all make sense and it will all be lies.

You have to decide who to trust. I did, and again, in my weakness, it looks like I have chosen wrong.

It is too soon to say that for sure, I tell myself, biting at my lip. By the time I do know, it will be too late. It seems important that I do something, although I have no idea what, and the best course of action is likely for me to wait in my quarters for Meredith's return. Aeida's unseen presence is like a bomb waiting to go off in my mind. It has unsettled me, and I am now seeing things where there is nothing to see, nothing to worry about. I can only wait for Meredith to come back, hopefully with good news about her Acolyte.

None of this is reassuring in the least, but reluctantly I head upstairs, intending to go to my quarters with some thought of asking Ana if she might know where Meredith is. As I pass down the hallway from the stairwell, I pause to knock on Meredith's door again. My hand is raised but it never descends, remaining in midair as I look back the way I came. Morris is not guarding the door to the Grand Regent's chambers. I take a step in that direction, even as my every instinct tells me to get as far away as possible as fast as I can.

My body is in there. And who knows what else. There is something very wrong with all of this.

Two things happen nearly at once. The elevator dings, announcing its impending arrival on this floor, and the stairwell door is thrown wide open, with Suon and De Vroes bursting forth. Suon runs toward me, her face taut with worry, sweat dripping down her cheek. De Vroes turns to face the opening elevator. He has a pulse pistol, I realize dimly. Two Black Robes begin to step out of the elevator and the renegade Acolyte greets them with blasts from the pistol, sending them both sprawling to the floor.

"Laila?" Suon says, gasping for breath as she reaches me.

I give her a slight, distracted nod, my eyes still on De Vroes. One of the Travelers is lying across the open elevator door, which is loudly beeping its intent to close. De Vroes quickly steps within and inserts a key to lock the elevator. He drags the two Black Robes within, collecting their weapons.

"Watch the other doors," he calls out.

"We have to go, Laila," Suon says, looking at the indicators above the remaining elevators to see if any of the others are rising. "The Society is here."

I blink at her, struggling to comprehend. "What's going on?"

"It's a Traveler raid. It has to be Molijc. He tipped them off somehow. They knew our positions and came right for us."

"That's impossible," I say, my mind still refusing to process what it is seeing.

"Look around," Suon says, pointing at the fallen Travelers.

"We have to move," De Vroes says as he joins us in the corridor.

"Laila?" Suon says, looking at me imploringly. "I know you don't trust us, but you don't want to be taken by the Society."

"They'll put you in a detention site and let the two of you fight it out until there's no mind left in you," De Vroes says.

That appears to be my fate no matter where I go. But they are correct, as much as I don't want to trust them. I think of the Seeker and how he wanted the Church destroyed. Perhaps this raid is his doing. He knows where I am, has to have known all along. So why authorize a raid now? What has changed?

"This may not be Molijc," I say, feeling trapped as both of them stare at me.

"It doesn't matter who it is," Suon says. "The Society is here. We have to go now."

"Why are you here?" I say, my suspicion of the two of them bringing my mind into focus.

"She insisted," De Vroes says, making clear that it is not his idea. "It'll probably get us all adjoining cells in a black site."

"We have to go," Suon says, putting a gentle hand on

my arm.

"Not without my body," I say, starting toward the Grand Regent's chambers.

"There's no time for that. The Black Robes will send someone else up here to investigate any second now." De Vroes is irate.

I glare at him. "What do you propose? We head down the stairs? Or take the elevator?"

"Do you have a better idea?"

"Yes," I say. "Do you think someone as paranoid as Molijc didn't have an escape route planned?"

"You know it?" Suon says, nodding toward the bank of elevators. One car has begun to rise from the ground floor, the numbers slowly increasing.

"Yes," I lie. "One of you go to my quarters and get Ana, if she's still there. I'm not leaving without her. I'll retrieve my body. We'll meet in the audience chamber."

Suon and De Vroes share a glance and a decision is made in an instant. "You go," De Vroes says. "I'll stay and handle this. Is there another way to the Grand Regent's chambers?"

I shake my head, already turning to go. De Vroes mutters something, taking up a position in the hallway out of sight of the rising elevator, while Suon runs to my door. I don't look back again, heading into the audience chamber, where I find De Gofroy sitting on the throne. He looks at me, his eyes glassy and unfocused, his face colored by bruises, and smiles triumphantly.

I ignore him, passing from the audience chamber to the interior rooms behind, heading down the corridor to my old quarters. At the door I hesitate, fearful that Molijc may have taken my body with him when he fled, not wanting to face that disappointment after so dislocating a morning. The sound of pulse weapons echoing through the walls spurs me on.

Inside my old quarters, I find myself lying upon the bed, exactly as I left me, awake but not aware. I stare at my body, unsure what to say or do. How to talk to myself. It feels ridiculous and deeply unsettling at the same time. My true fear is that someone else is in there, existing as I do in a foreign body, unable to ever feel truly themselves.

Another volley of pulse fire spurs me to action, and I reach out to grasp myself by the arm and shake myself awake. I sit up in bed and look in my direction, though my eyes don't seem to focus on anything in particular. The blankness that is there in all the half-things is even more visible here. I want to scream, seeing myself like this, unable to do anything about it.

Instead, I take a deep breath. "Come on," I say. "It's time to go."

I get to my feet, eager to comply and follow behind as I make my way back to the audience chamber, wondering as I go why I didn't have the sense to take one of the pulse weapons with me. Not that De Vroes offered me one. He doesn't trust me, which oddly reassures me. It is Suon, desperate as always to gain my faith, who I am suspicious of.

We arrive in the audience room just as Suon, De Vroes, and Ana scramble in and slam the door behind them.

"There's more coming," De Vroes says. "Can we lock this damn door?"

"The throne," I say, as they both struggle to find the locking mechanism. There is one, but it is electronic, and Molijc will have changed the codes.

Suon runs from the door to join me by the throne where De Gofroy still sits.

"It is mine," he announces to us, sitting up tall.

"Get out, you old fool," I say.

Suon grabs him by the shoulder and drags him off the chair, spilling him on the floor. Together we try to carry it to the door, but it is so heavy that we can barely get it off the dais. There are shouts from outside as another elevator filled with Black Robes arrives.

"What the fuck is this built with?" Suon says, panic

breaking her voice.

"Come on," I say to myself and Ana, gesturing for them to help. They come, eager to comply, and the four of us are able to move the throne to the door. We arrive just as the Black Robes do on the other side. One of them tries the door handle, which De Vroes holds tight while we position the chair.

"There's people in here," the Black Robe calls to his fellows. "Cease and desist," he shouts to us in a ringing, authoritative voice. "You are under arrest by the Society of Travelers for violating the laws of the Society. You will immediately surrender your weapons and place yourselves into our custody."

He is pushing against the door, fighting a battle with De Vroes over the handle, as he shouts. We maneuver the back of the chair up so that De Vroes can step aside and the throne will block the door. The door lurches open a little before the throne stops it and the Black Robe on the other side gives a grunt of triumph. He reaches in with one hand to try to see what is blocking the doorway. As he does so, the four of us put our weight against the chair in unison.

There is a scream of shock and horror on the other side of the door. The hand that was inside the room disappears, though there is blood on the doorframe and the throne. The door itself is closed, the throne firmly against it.

"That won't give us long," De Vroes says, as we all gather our breath.

"We don't need long," I say, hoping that is true.

I run to the wall that conceals the doorway to the study and spring the mechanism opening it. Molijc's escape route has to be hidden somewhere within, I am convinced. This is why he slept here, rather than in his own quarters, after Osahi arrived. He wanted to be able to flee at a moment's notice. Because he knew this day was coming, one way or another.

In the corridor, the Black Robes have regrouped and begun to throw their weight against the door. The throne moves almost imperceptibly, the door still not open. Soon enough, it will be.

23

As the thud of the Black Robes' shoulders against the door continues at the calm, steady pace of agents certain of their eventual triumph, I motion for everyone to follow me inside the study. "Bring him too," I say, pointing at De Gofroy. "We don't want him telling them where we've gone."

When everyone has crowded within, I close the door. The study looks much the same as the last time I saw it. There is a cot in the corner and dirty dishes and various papers litter the desk, while the floor has shirts and underwear spread about. It is a pathetic scene in so many ways, evidence of a meager life lived on the run. Except the Grand Regent was not on the run—he was situated at the heart of his power, where his authority was absolute.

That is not what I see here. This is life of a hunted man. Molijc acted as though each day might be his last of freedom. There is something significant in that, though exactly what it is, I am unsure.

Everyone is looking at me expectantly. I bite my lip and look around the room, trying to recall the floor plans for the tower and which wall Molijc could have put another door in. So much has changed since I was last here that it could be anywhere. Perhaps it is not here at all and I have guessed wrong, and we will be trapped in this little room, waiting for the Travelers to discover us.

I notice a half-drunk cup of coffee on the desk and find it is still warm to the touch. I press my fingers to it as though it might be able to guide me to where Molijc went when the raid began. It happened very quickly, in the time it took me to go downstairs and back up again. The still-warm coffee suggests that Molijc found himself overtaken by events and forced to leave in a hurry.

Outside, the thud of shoulders against the door gets louder. It will not take them long to work the chair back enough for someone to slip through the door and into the audience chamber. I force myself to breathe and try to still the flurry of my thoughts.

"Where is the way out?" De Vroes says in a loud voice.

"Quiet," I say. "They don't know about this place and they won't find it so long as we don't make any noise."

De Vroes looks as though he is about to argue with me, but mercifully, he bites his tongue. The groan of the throne against the floor, followed by a shout of triumph, tells us the Black Robes are in the audience room. Everyone goes very still, their eyes upon the door, looks of dread on their faces. I point at De Gofroy, making it clear to De Vroes and Suon that they need to keep an eye on him and make sure he stays quiet.

Everything now depends on the Society being unaware of this study and the hidden door mechanism. I am fairly confident in that regard. Aside from Molijc and De Gofroy, Meredith is likely the only one here who is aware of its existence. Perhaps the half-Morris as well, but both are likely with Molijc, fleeing the campus grounds. Lasinha could be added to that list, but he is banished and gone and unlikely to be at the target of a Society raid. The Black Robes may find it eventually, but only after they have conducted a search of the entire floor.

By then we should be gone. Assuming I can find

Molijc's escape.

With sudden intuition, I look at myself and lean across to whisper in my ear. "Where is the door? Where did he go?"

A cloud passes over my eyes, an internal struggle taking place, between my innate desire to do as asked and a previous order. Which will win out?

The room is growing stifling with so many people crammed into such a small space. Outside we can hear the Black Robes pulling aside the throne to give them better access to the audience chamber. Orders are being shouted to conduct a thorough search.

"It's okay," I say, my voice barely audible even to myself. "The Grand Regent told me to bring you to him in the event you were separated from him in an emergency."

Why the Grand Regent didn't bother to tell me the location of his secret escape route is something that I will have to explain should the question come. Fortunately, the Acolytes have done their work well, and my enfeebled self does not think to ask it. The cloud of thought goes from my eyes, and I look to the corner where the safe with De Gofroy's files once sat.

I squeeze my way through those gathered and begin to feel around the wall for the outline of a door. None is apparent, no matter how many times I run my fingers over the paint. I can feel everyone watching me, their fear mounting by the moment as they begin to wonder if they've made a terrible mistake following me in here. I am wondering it myself. The air around us is thick and warm and feels like a noose being drawn tighter around my throat with each breath.

"What is the meaning of this?" De Gofroy says, as though he has just realized something is going on. He speaks in a normal voice, but it sounds like a shout in the stifling quiet of the study.

De Vroes is the closest, and he reacts with brutal swiftness, landing a blow with the butt of his pistol on De

Gofroy's temple. A delayed look of surprise flashes across De Gofroy's face and his mouth opens as though he is about to say something. Instead it hangs there, and he lets out an odd sigh as his legs collapse under him. Suon is prepared behind him, catching him and helping to the floor. She stays crouched over him, ready to act should he try to speak again, though he appears unconscious.

The rest of us go even stiller, if such a thing is possible. Even Ana and my enfeebled self seem to recognize the nature of our predicament as we wait to see whether anyone has heard De Gofroy's outburst in the audience chamber. I count off the seconds, straining to hear if anyone is approaching the other side of the wall. If they are, they are being very quiet.

I turn back to the corner of the room, abandoning my search of the wall, and look at the floor. The carpet there appears unbroken, but as I run my fingers along it, I am certain I can feel seams where it comes apart and lifts away. I dig my fingers into where I think one is, but the carpet will not separate. There must be some mechanism, a trigger or a lock somewhere, as with the door to the audience room. But what sort of mechanism, and where is it hidden?

A rap at the wall behind us makes everyone jump and gasp, the sound of our breath like thunderclaps. The tapping at the wall continues and is followed by a pair of muffled voices—a question and then a response. De Vroes raises his pulse weapon, aiming it at the still-closed door, and Suon does the same a moment later. I take a deep breath, telling myself not to panic, to take my time, and turn back to the floor.

I run my hands over the carpet, my fingers feeling the seams again, but finding no way to release the lock. It is only on my third time passing over that I find a loose strand of carpet, barely visible even from my vantage point hunched over the floor. I dig around the carpet nearby, pulling at the strand, and at last find the piece that comes away, revealing a catch. Turning it makes the floor lift up, air hissing at the release. There are handles, and I pull the floor away, as gently as possible to muffle the noise. Below I can see darkness and the first rungs of a ladder.

I stick my head into the hole, trying to make out what lies below, but there is only darkness. The tapping at the wall ceases, and we all turn from the open hatch to the door, certain that it is about to open. It doesn't, and there is a shout—an order—from somewhere in the room. The tapping does not resume.

Whether they have abandoned the search, or simply gone to get equipment to take down the wall, I don't wait to see. I stand and wave for everyone to go down the ladder. Suon goes first, followed by Ana and myself. De Vroes and I look at each other and then De Gofroy, lying on the floor. The renegade Acolyte nudges him with his toe, but the unconscious man doesn't stir. With a nod to me, De Vroes starts down the ladder.

I wait for him to descend, cocking my head to try to hear what is happening in the audience chamber. There are muffled sounds, all indistinct, and I am unable to glean any clues from them. I follow behind De Vroes, sealing the hatch above. Darkness surrounds me and I descend slowly, not wanting to step on De Vroes' fingers. The air here is even more stifling than the study was, hardly a surprise given there can be no airflow reaching this shaft, and I am soon dripping with sweat.

The darkness and the oppressive heat give me a deep sense of claustrophobia and an irrational feeling that we are descending into a furnace. This is made worse by the narrowness of the shaft, which is barely an arm's length across. I have to stay close to the ladder as I descend to avoid touching the wall behind me. Doing so results in a small cloud of drywall or other building material being sent into the air. I inhale a little and immediately feel a desperate need to sneeze or cough, something I want to avoid, given I don't know if there are Travelers on the other side of the wall.

At the bottom of the ladder, which I estimate has taken us down three floors, there is a corridor, almost as narrow as the shaft. Ahead of me I can see forms and a glimmer of light. I go forward, tapping De Vroes on the shoulder and slipping past the others. Suon has a cell phone out and is casting it along the wall at the corridor's end, looking for some kind of door. There is none apparent, the wall seeming like any other wall.

Typical fucking Molijc, I think, shaking my head. Never one secret door when three will do.

I step in front of Suon, gesturing for her to hold up the cell phone to provide me with light, and begin to run my fingers along all three walls at the end of the corridor. There is a cough from someone behind me that freezes me and everyone else, visions of Black Robes descending from above, stalking our every breath, filling our minds. My hands are trembling as I begin my search again, which is concerning for a whole host of reasons, none of which I can afford to contemplate now.

The door is hidden in the wall to the right, a little bit down from the corridor's end. It is obvious at the touch that this section is not made from drywall, as it has been made to appear. A light tap suggests metal of some sort. An elevator is my first thought. I wonder what Watchers built this and how long it was after they finished that the Acolytes came for them. Molijc is, if nothing else, thorough.

As I search for the mechanism, muffled shouts reach us from down the shaft. The Black Robes have made their way into the study and perhaps even discovered the hatch that leads here.

"Unbelievable," I say under my breath in frustration as I desperately run my hands along the wall and then the floor. There is nothing anywhere I can find that would act as a trigger to unlock the door and reveal whatever lies behind it.

I step back to gather my thoughts and try to calm myself. De Vroes mutters something, retreats along the corridor, and comes back shaking his head. It is unclear whether that means the ladder and tunnel are empty or that the Black Robes have breached the hatch and are descending. I turn my attention back to the wall, trying to will it into revealing its secrets, but none appear.

Suon touches my shoulder and points up at the ceiling, shining her phone at what looks like a tiny smoke detector. There is a bit of pipe running to it along the ceiling, but I can think of no purpose for it. I reach up and try to pull the cover off, but it refuses to budge. It will turn, though, and I twist it counterclockwise until it clicks into place.

We all wait, but nothing happens. Above there is another cry, still muffled and indistinct, but it feels closer than before. I reach up to the false detector and try to turn it again, but it will not go forward. Instead I return it to its original position. There is another satisfying click and the detector begins to slide into the ceiling. I push it until it locks into place and am exultant to see the doors to an elevator, hidden behind the false paneling of the wall, open before me.

It is a small elevator, meant for one or two people, but the five of us crowd in. There is no floor to select, and we let the doors close and begin our lurching journey below.

24

The elevator ride passes in an uneasy silence, all of us looking at each other for guidance. Even Ana and myself seem unsettled. The elevator car vibrates as it descends, and I have visions of our weight shaking it loose from its cables. To avoid thinking of that, I try to determine where in the building Molijc would have the elevator stop. What would give him the best chance of escaping? There is only one answer: the tunnels.

The elevator comes to an abrupt halt, jolting us, pitching me into my own arms. I jerk myself free, shuddering with horror, while Suon looks at me with concern on her face. Though I want to give her a cutting remark, I do not. The Travelers could be anywhere on the campus, even in the tunnels, so we need to stay quiet to avoid discovery.

When the door opens, I let Suon and De Vroes exit first, their weapons raised and ready to fire. They peer down either end of a dimly lit corridor before waving at us that it is safe to come out. The three of us emerge from the elevator, glancing about tentatively to get our bearings. Behind us, the elevator doors close and are hidden behind another seamless false panel that blends into the surrounding wall.

Briefly I consider finding the mechanism to open it again and trying to disable the elevator to stop the Travelers from following us, before deciding against it. We have no tools to break into the panel within the elevator, and, even if we could manage that, it would take valuable time that we don't have. There is more than one way into this tunnel, as is made clear by the fact it stretches off in either direction for an indeterminate distance, and the Black Robes will have the means to find the other entrances.

That leaves aside the fact that they may be able to track us with the equipment available to them. Even if the traces of our most recent transfer have dissipated, which I am uncertain of, Suon and the body I occupy are not of this universe. They may have equipment that would let them find people like us. If they don't, a Seeker undoubtedly can. In spite of what Suon and De Vroes claimed about Molijc being behind the raid, I cannot help but see the Seeker's hand. It was only a matter of time before he sought me out and made me honor our bargain.

I say none of this to either of them. If there is a Seeker here, the Travelers will find us. All we can do is run and hope for the best.

Everyone is looking at me again for guidance as to which direction we should take, and so I push these doubts aside and focus on the problem at hand. Immediately I can see that the corridor we find ourselves in is not one of the network of tunnels which I am familiar with that lie under the campus. The lighting is completely different, softer and more diffuse, and the tunnel itself is of newer construction, with none of the exposed conduits that marked the older corridors.

Molijc built this specifically as an escape route, which means it is unlikely that it connects back into the main set of tunnels. The fact that the corridor stretches in two directions suggests a few possibilities. One is that he wanted to confuse any possible pursuit, another that he wanted several options as to where he would emerge from underground, depending on the situation he found himself in.

But how are we to choose which is the best to take? There is no way to know. I turn to myself and point to the left of the elevator. "Where does that go?"

I shrug and shake my head. My voice seems to echo down the corridors, sounding impossibly loud, and I can see Suon and De Vroes wincing and looking over their shoulders as if they are expecting Travelers to emerge from the darkness at the sound.

I point the other direction. "And that?" I say, dropping my voice to a whisper.

"The hospital," I say, with confidence.

"You've been that way before?"

I nod. "Yes."

"Inside the hospital?" De Vroes says. I understand his confusion. The physical plant building marks the southwestern corner of the campus. To the west of it, just down the street, is a children's hospital that, to the best of my knowledge, is still in use, even with Calgary's rapid depopulation following the arrival of the Travelers and all that went with it, including the collapse of the oil economy that the city depended on.

"Inside it," I say with certainty.

I look at De Vroes and Suon. "What do you think?"

"I think we go that way," Suon says. "We at least have some idea of where we're going to end up. And the Travelers will be reluctant to get in a firefight in a hospital."

De Vroes nods, and I do too, though I don't share Suon's confidence that the hospital will protect us from the Black Robes. They have no one to answer to here. I turn to myself. "Lead the way."

I nod and smile, starting forward down the corridor. Ana moves to follow, and Suon does as well, though she stops beside me to whisper in my ear.

"Are you sure you trust her? Molijc might have left her behind for a reason. She could be leading us into a trap."

"I don't see as we have any other choice," I say, not bothering to add that I fear whoever is pursuing us far more than whatever traps Molijc has left in his wake.

Suon shrugs and moves on ahead, leaving De Vroes and I to follow behind. He hands me one of the pulse weapons he picked up from a fallen Black Robe and tucks his own into his belt and under his shirt.

"Best to do the same," he says. "Don't want any alarms raised at the hospital."

I nod, copying him in slipping the pistol into the back of my pants. We carry on in silence, periodically glancing back when we hear an odd sound. Mostly these are just the hum of a fan being switched on or the gurgle of pipes passing somewhere nearby. There is no sign of pursuit, at least not that I can hear, and gradually I find the tension that has held tight across my chest since De Vroes and Suon arrived atop the tower relaxing.

It is dangerous to do so, I know, for while the threat might not appear immediate, it is not far away. We cannot run forever—no one can from the Society.

After fifteen minutes, we arrive at the end of the corridor. There is a door with a keypad lock requiring a PIN code to open it. Everyone looks at me, and I look at myself.

"Do you know it?" I say, and I shake my head.

Sighing, I enter the old code to the tunnels, the one that Molijc reinstated knowing I would be returning. It fails, as I knew it would. I ponder the keypad, wondering if I can hack into it and override the PIN. Given enough time, probably, but how much time do we have?

"Any ideas?" I say, glancing back at Suon and De Vroes.

Both of them shake their head. "If we'd had time, I would have grabbed some equipment to let us hack into the system," Suon says, stepping forward to peer at the keypad. "I'd be worried about tripping an alarm if we tried it now. It would lock us in here and we'd be fucked."

"That may be our only choice," De Vroes says. "Unless you can guess it?"

"How many tries do we get?" Suon asks.

I shake my head. "Three probably, so we have two left."

De Vroes winces, and we all look at the keypad as though it might somehow reveal its secrets.

"I guess we try to hack it," Suon says.

I shrug and am about to agree with her when a dim voice reaches us from down the corridor. We all whirl around and peer to where the dim light dissolves into a kind of darkness, obscuring whatever lies there. Another voice follows the first, curt and abrupt, and silence is restored.

De Vroes swallows. "How far away?"

"Not far enough," I say. Both of us are whispering, our voices pitched so low that Ana and myself will not be able to hear. I don't know how well the corridor carries sound, but I'm hoping they are at least five minutes away. Though I don't know why—it's not as though it will make any difference, unless I can guess the PIN.

"Do you think they heard us?" Suon says.

De Vroes shrugs. "They know we came here. Our best chance is they've had to divide their forces, but that won't buy us much time once the shooting starts. The whole damn Society will be here."

Our best chance was if I could guess Molijc's code, but I don't bother saying that. I turn back and look at the keypad, trying to recall other codes that we used in the past, weighing whether he might use them. In the end, I reject them all. He no longer trusts Lasinha, and Lasinha will have known of this escape route and all the codes. There is the final day of the Uayeb when the Grand Regent died and we seized control of the Church, or the date when Molijc ascended to the Grand Regency. Both have enough digits for the code, but both are also too obvious. They are the first thing to my mind, and presumably Lasinha's as well.

The sound of footsteps down the corridor appears, intruding on my thoughts. I turn from the keypad to look down the corridor with everyone else, but there is no sign of anyone yet. They will be there soon, though. De Vroes and Suon take their pulse weapons out and move a little down the tunnel, aiming them so they are ready to fire as soon as the Travelers are in sight.

As he goes, De Vroes says, "Just pick something."

I do. Dates seem to be in my mind, the only numbers I can think of that might appeal to Molijc. I choose the date that he joined the Church, or at least what I remember it was from De Gofroy's files. It doesn't work, the light on the keypad flashing a grim red. I turn and look back at Suon and De Vroes, crouched and ready to fire. Ana and myself are crouched down too, pressed against the wall in the vain hope that will help them avoid being shot.

I turn back to the keypad. One more chance. It is probably not a date, probably just a random string of numbers. That would be safest and would be what Lasinha or I would choose. Molijc was always different, though. He wanted a message in a code, a reminder to whoever entered it of their place in the Church or in relation to him. Now though he wants something that I will not guess, something that he thinks would never occur to Lasinha or I.

One such date comes to mind. The day we first met, the day Lasinha and De Gofroy sent me to him and him to me. It is just the sort of thing Molijc would do, knowing I might try to follow him when he fled. I don't think about it a moment further and enter the date on the keypad. It chimes recognition and the lock on the door clicks open.

I gasp in relief, so loudly it startles me, and pull the door open, waving myself and Ana through. De Vroes and

Suon scamper after them, never taking their eyes off the empty corridor, which I expect to be filled any moment by the figures behind the approaching footsteps. I remain hunched over the keypad, frantically trying to recode it. If I can set it to trigger an alarm once the Black Robes try to override it, the whole corridor will lock down, making it more difficult for them to hack the lock and buying us a little time.

"Come on, Laila," Suon says in an earnest voice, and both of us look up at her, my half-self in confusion, me in irritation.

"Cover me," I say, though there is no cover where I am standing.

Suon crouches behind the wall beside the door, only her pulse pistol visible and pointing at the empty corridor. Behind her I can hear De Vroes calling in an angry voice for me to get my fucking ass in gear. As he says that, I hear a shout from down the corridor as one of the Black Robes sees me. Suon lets off a couple of quick bursts of her pistol, and I hear a cry of agony and shouts to fall back.

I try to ignore it all, punching in commands on the keypad. One of the Black Robes returns Suon's fire, the heat of the pulse passing near my head. I duck instinctively, crouching low so that I am looking up at the keypad. More shots follow, scattered around me, none as close. Suon keeps up her suppressing fire, holding them far enough away that their aim is compromised.

"For fuck's sake, just leave her," De Vroes says. "We're going to have the whole Society here in a second."

Suon doesn't stir from her position, still firing off shots. I grimace and prepare a retort, as I punch in the PIN one last time to authorize my command. The words do not come to my lips. The world is black and spinning and color all at once.

25

Pain burns through the ends of my fingers. They are vibrating out of time with the rest of me. I open my eyes and see blue sky, glorious and vast, and a spinning sun descending toward me. Closer and closer. I try to sit up, to flee from the falling star, and groan in agony. All my muscles feel like they are stretched tight, nearly torn from the bones they are attached to.

"Lie down. Lie down. Don't move. You took a pulse shot."

A woman's voice. Familiar. My mind tries to place it as I work to focus my eyes upon her face. Everything is scattered there and incoherent.

"Suon, we need to get moving." A man's voice, harsh and under strain.

"Look at her. She can't go anywhere."

"Then we leave her. I'm not chancing getting caught by the Society just to save her. Do you know the things she's done?"

"No worse than you. Or any of us."

I start to explain to them about my fingers, how they are vibrating out of sync with the rest of me, but the woman puts a hand to my chest. "Easy, easy," she says.

She is whispering now, and the other man is silent. My eyes slowly come into focus and I can see her, kneeling beside me, looking away from me, as though someone or something is approaching. The man returns, and I recognize De Vroes. His expression is grim and strained.

"We can't risk staying any longer," he says quietly, crouching on the other side of me.

Suon—it is Suon—looks at me and then at the Acolyte. "Where do we go?"

De Vroes considers the question. "I think we head south. There's an old park there. It's overgrown now. Even if they can track us somehow, it'll be tough for them to find us in there. At least it will buy us some time, let her recover. We can't stay here, though. We're too near the hospital and the campus, and we're too exposed."

"Right," Suon says, and looks down at me. "Do you think you can move? It's not far."

"I can try," I say, feeling confused, but understanding the urgency of the situation from her voice. Though I am still not sure whether I trust her. Or De Vroes. Despite the fact that they appear to be helping me now, they may have an ulterior motive. I cannot forget that.

I struggle to my feet with Suon's help, my muscles going into spasms that make me gasp.

"It's just the pulse," Suon says. "It'll pass soon enough. We're lucky they had them set to stun."

I nod. She slips underneath my shoulder, putting her arm around my back, bearing some of weight. "Okay?" she says, looking at me. I nod, though even that hurts. She looks to De Vroes, and he leads the way. Each step is an effort, and I keep my eyes concentrated on the ground to ensure I don't stumble. Suon squeezes my shoulder in encouragement, and I resist a shudder.

I don't trust her. I have no memory of being shot, and I don't know where we are or where they are taking me. Or to what end.

As we move forward, I realize there are two others

with us. I look around wildly, trying to see who is there, and nearly send both Suon and myself to the ground. "Easy, easy," she whispers. I nod, trying to steady my breathing, which is ragged. One of the figures comes into view beside me, and I see it is Ana and feel a rush of relief, though I'm not certain why. She will be little help to me, and we may both be pawns in Suon and the Acolyte's game.

I catch glimpses of scenery from the corner of my eyes. Anonymous buildings, snatches of greenery. Empty parking lots overgrown by weeds and grass. None of it looks remotely familiar. We must be off the campus, I realize, and wonder how we made it past the cordon of Watchers. I try to turn around to see what is behind us, but Suon doesn't let me.

"Easy, Laila," she murmurs in my ear.

I frown and glance at her, a retort on my lips, but I manage to hold myself in check. Time enough for that when I have recovered. For now, I am relying on both her and De Vroes. Besides, they have guns. I can see one tucked into De Vroes' belt, the outline just visible through his shirt.

By the time we arrive at what is apparently our destination, I have recovered somewhat. Walking is no longer agony and my body no longer feels as though it is moving at different frequencies, pulling itself apart at the seams. My thoughts are clear, as well as my senses. I feel myself, if such a thing is even possible for me now. Likely not.

De Vroes calls us to a halt somewhere in the middle of what, according to him, is a park. It looks more look a forest to me, grown over with trees and bushes, with grass that reaches up past my waist. None of the trees is particularly tall or thick, though there are a variety of them, all prairie stock, not like the vast rainforest trees I am used to. I can see no reason why De Vroes has chosen this place to stop, except that the trees are particularly thick here, and the tangle of their leafy branches will obscure any view of us from overhead.

As we sit down to rest at the base of the trees, I get a shock. There is an additional member of our party, who I had not noticed. She must have been walking behind Suon and I the entire time. It is Laila. My surprise—and the hate I cannot control that rises at the very thought of her—must be visible on my face, for Suon reacts immediately.

"It's not Laila," she says, frantic, getting to her feet.

I grimace. "No," I say, before I falter, trying and failing to find some explanation.

Suon looks to De Vroes for help, and he stands. I get to my feet unsteadily, holding out forestalling hands.

"I'm Laila," I say, sounding unconvincing even to my own ears. "I just got shaken up by the pulse shot."

"Can you get her back?" Suon says, ignoring me and looking at De Vroes.

"Maybe," he says. "If you're right, and she was using dampeners, I can see if I can stabilize her. But it may not work."

"That bitch," I say, unable to help myself. Dampeners. That is why I have such scattered memories these last days, however many there have been. What has she been doing all this time?

I am already moving away from Suon and De Vroes, heading deeper into the park, though I have no idea where it leads. Suon gives a shout of frustration and De Vroes pulls his pulse weapon. "Don't think I won't shoot you, Aeida." I ignore him and keep moving, though it is still difficult and painful. There is no way I will be able to outrun them.

I hardly make it past the circle of trees we are under before I am tackled to the ground. The air goes from my chest, and I fight to breathe. Rolling over, I see Ana, looking down at me with her blank, unquestioning face. I yell out in frustration. De Vroes and Suon are already there, crouching over me.

"Shut him up," Suon says. "Half of Calgary can hear him yelling."

De Vroes ignores her. He has a syringe from somewhere and a bottle of some drug that he is filling it with. "Hold him," he says, as I struggle. The rest of them pin me down while he injects me and the world turns black.

26

I come to with a gasp, as though I was drowning, water pressing heavily against my lungs. My breathing is ragged and panicked, and when I try to get up, everything hurts. For a moment I wonder if I was, in fact, drowning. But all my clothes are dry and the sun is shining above through the trees. It is a warm, idyllic day, a perfect afternoon to luxuriate in the sun.

It takes me some time to regain my bearings. The others are watching me warily—De Vroes and Suon, at least—as if they are waiting to see what I will do. I cough and look at Suon, who eyes me imploringly, as though willing me to be the person she wants me to be. But I am not, and I do not trust her. She is still Osahi's, after all.

"What's going on?" I manage to say. "Where are we?"

"Laila?" Suon says tentatively.

I put a hand to my head, which aches horribly. There is a drumming there in time with my pulse. "He came back, did he?"

"After you were shot," Suon says, in a gentle voice. "De Vroes applied a suppressant."

"It should keep him quiet for a while," De Vroes says. "Though I can't say for sure how long. I don't know how big of a mess you've made of things in there. Dampeners are not to be toyed with."

"Everyone else seems to be playing with my mind. I figured I should join the party."

De Vroes smiles grimly. "I can certainly understand not wanting him around anymore. But it was dangerous. Who knows what the result might have been. Or was, for that matter."

I sigh and close my eyes. My headache seems to ease a little. "There were some unintended consequences, no doubt. What's our situation?"

"We're in the old park just south of the hospital and the physical plant," Suon says. "It looks like you managed to get the Travelers who were following us stuck in the tunnel. No one followed us out and no one followed us in here."

I open my eyes. "That's good. They may still be able to track us."

De Vroes nods. "I figure they can. But only to a point. If we're in here, it should make it a little more difficult for them to pinpoint us from the airships. It will take a lot of manpower to sweep this park, and we don't know whether they can spare it. Or if they will bother."

"They will," I say, thinking of the Seeker.

"They don't know who they were chasing," Suon says. "If they have Osahi and his top people, they may have all that they're looking for. Assuming they cut some deal with Molijc to let him make a getaway."

"I don't believe Molijc had anything to do with this," I say. "He would do almost anything to stop Osahi, but he would never invite the Black Robes onto campus. He's always been paranoid about them, and that's only gotten worse since we were arrested. It's poisoned him."

"I don't know, Laila," Suon says, before stopping herself.

De Vroes shakes his head. "Is it just coincidence he disappeared as soon as the airships arrived? I don't think so. Was it chance the Black Robes stormed Osahi's positions on the sixth floor first? Not the tower. Not the main floor or the second floor. That's how we were able to get away." He looks at Suon. "Somebody told them where to go. And it benefitted Molijc directly."

"Did it?" I say, getting to my feet and drawing a look of worry from Suon. "In the short term, maybe. But the Society will have taken all the half-things he had to leave behind. The High Regents. The others. How much does the Society really know about what you're doing?"

De Vroes looks evasive, parsing his words carefully. "They've some idea, I'm sure. There are enough rumors out there among the faithful about what the Order is doing. But they don't know how or why necessarily."

"With the half-things and whatever else they can find on campus—transfer equipment, whatever it may be—they could arrest the entire Hierarchy. Or what's left of it, anyway."

"They don't need evidence to arrest us," De Vroes says. "It didn't stop them before. The Church hadn't even started crossing over at that point. If they wanted to arrest you, to shut down the whole Church, they could do it. But they haven't."

"I know," I say.

"But have you really thought about why that is? Really?"

I have, but I don't say anything further. Whatever my conclusions are, they will remain mine. I still do not trust these two, though they have both undeniably aided me today, at great risk to themselves. The question there, too, is why? And again, I have many thoughts on the matter, but precious few definitive answers.

I walk about the clearing, testing my legs to see how they will respond. The pain has gone for the most part, replaced by a numbness that seems to create a field extending just beyond my skin. Every step feels precarious, and I cannot entirely trust the sensations coming from my legs. But after a bit of walking about, the feeling returns and I regain some confidence that I will be able to run should the Black Robes come.

As I make my circuits through the trees, Ana comes to join me. She smiles at me and lifts up her blouse to reveal a small hard drive tucked into the belt of her pants. I stare at it incredulously, knowing what it is and yet unable to comprehend how she came to possess it.

"I brought this for you," she says. "I thought you would want to bring it."

"Thank you, Ana," I say, taking it from her, sliding it into the front pocket of my jeans, where it sits uncomfortably.

"What is that?" Suon says.

"The past," I say, drawing stares from both her and De Vroes. "Does one of you want to come with me?"

Suon stands to go while De Vroes doesn't move. "Where exactly?" he says.

"To the edge of the park. I want to see what the situation is on campus with the Black Robes."

"No. What if they see you? We can't risk that."

"They can find us if they want to, no matter where we go. Have you thought about why they haven't bothered?" I stare a challenge at De Vroes. He shakes his head. "I don't know either. But I intend to find out."

I head off toward the campus, not checking to see if De Vroes has any further objections. He raises none, and Suon falls in beside me. We make our way through the trees, which grow so tightly clustered together that we are forced to double back and find other paths through. We pause in places to listen and see if we can hear anyone else moving through the park. All we hear are birdsong and insects and the breeze stirring the tall grass and branches. At one point I hear the song of a meadowlark and feel a deep pang of nostalgia. How long has it been since I heard one sing? It feels like it must have been my childhood, though I know that can't be true.

We come across the remnants of an old path through the park and follow it as best we can the rest of the way. When the trees began to thin and we can glimpse the road that borders the campus, we go down on our hands and knees and crawl forward the rest of the way to make certain that no one sees or hears our approach. At the park's edge, we take cover behind a bush and peer out across the road. There is no one in sight and no sign of any presence, Traveler, Watcher, or otherwise.

After waiting several minutes, just to be certain that a patrol has not been set up, I stand up and move to get a better view of the campus along the road. Suon makes a small sound of protest beside me before following. From our vantage point we can see the physical plant, shaded behind a row of trees, and a few of the old residence buildings for the initiates. The Watchers' cordon has vanished; even their vehicles are gone. They must have had some advance warning of the raid.

The only sign of any Society presence is a lone airship hovering above the Grand Regent's tower. "There were three," Suon says, following my gaze.

"Clearly they've got what they came for." I ponder the airship and look at Suon. "Why use airships? Very public. And very obvious that they're coming. The whole city will know they were here."

"It gave the Watchers lots of warning to get away, though," Suon says bitterly. "He cut a deal with them. The Grand Regent is in bed with the Travelers."

I open my mouth to argue, but realize there is no point. All the evidence points in that direction, whatever my instincts might tell me about how unbelievable it is. It can't be right, but it also doesn't matter. I am finished with this madness. There is only one thing left to do.

"Come on," I say, striding back into the trees. "There's something I need to ask De Vroes."

Suon doesn't say a word, but from her face I can tell that she knows what my question will be.

De Vroes and the half-things are in the same clearing, alert and watchful, when we return.

"You can put that thing away," I say, gesturing at De Vroes' gun. "The Black Robes aren't coming."

"Are you sure?" De Vroes says, though he lowers the weapon.

"Two of the airships are gone already. And there's no sign of any Travelers on this edge of the campus," Suon says, though she sounds doubtful.

"If they were coming, they would be here," I say. "They've gotten what they came for. Osahi's dream is done and Molijc is still Grand Regent. We're immaterial to that."

"We are," De Vroes says. "I'm not so sure about you."

I shrug and sit down next to Ana, who smiles at me.

"Maybe they didn't know you were here," Suon says. "Or that you were one of the people they were chasing. They might have just thought it was some of Osahi's people. No one important."

"Molijc does seem to care greatly about you still," De Vroes says. "In his way."

I raise an eyebrow, but do not dispute the point.

"You think he wanted to make certain she wasn't picked up in the raid?" Suon says, frowning.

"It's possible," I say. "But if he wanted me safe, why not take me with him when he fled?"

"True," De Vroes says, mulling that thought and picking at the grass at his feet, before looking up. "What do we do now?"

"I have some thoughts on that," I say, looking steadily at him. "I say we go back and see if the Black Robes have left anything behind."

"Too risky," De Vroes says, shaking his head.

"If they wanted us, they would have us," I say.

"That doesn't mean we should just hand ourselves to them."

"All I want to know is if any of your equipment is still there."

De Vroes looks surprised, his eyes narrowing. "What are you thinking?"

"You know what I am. Do you have everything there you need to do it?"

De Vroes sighs and looks at his hands. "Assuming it's all there and in one piece, yes. But there's no guarantee. Besides, I don't see why I should risk myself to help you."

"You're the one who's been saying you don't agree with what your brethren are doing," Suon says. "You left the guild. You were so against what the Acolytes were doing that you lost Osahi's trust. It cost you everything."

"It also saved me," De Vroes says in a matter-of-fact tone. "All of that is true, but it doesn't explain why I should help you."

"Help us," I say, gesturing to myself and Ana. "Now is your chance to set right some of the wrong they've done. You may not be able to stop the Acolytes from doing it to anyone else, but at least you can undo what has been done here."

"Her, I can definitely fix," he says, pointing at Ana. "You two...it's a little more complicated, I'm afraid. I don't know what, or who, is in her. And I've certainly never moved someone between bodies. I didn't even know it was possible until I met you. I'd be worried about doing real damage if I tried."

It is exactly what I feared he would say, but I try not to let my disappointment show. There is also Ibrahem to think about. He is an example of what can go wrong with procedure, and of De Vroes' own failure. But there is no safe path available for me. Or Ana. "You can still do something for Ana. Set that right, at least."

De Vroes looks away, out into the trees, still clearly reluctant. Suon sighs. "What else are we going to do now? Osahi's gone. We've lost. There's nothing left of the Church or the Acolytes, not that we could ever go back to.

We might as well try to do this."

"I have no appetite to be captured by the Travelers," De Vroes says.

"They're gone. Or they will be soon enough," I say. "All I want is to see if the equipment is there. If it is, then you try to restore Ana. If not, we all go wherever our paths take us."

He studies me closely, his fingers still pulling at tufts of grass. "Okay," he says, looking over at Ana. "For her sake, I will try. But if we see any sign of the Travelers, I'm gone."

"Good," I say with a grin that feels desperate. "We'll go tonight."

27

It is still daylight when the five of us leave the park and cross over onto the campus. Though it is late in the evening, summer is now near and the days in Calgary are getting long, the sun not setting until after nine. A peaceful calm holds sway over the campus, broken only by the distant sounds of traffic and the odd crow calling from one of the trees. We could be a group of friends out for a stroll, though none of us speaks and we are all on alert, uncertain what we will find in the Grand Regent's tower.

The campus is empty, the Travelers' final airship gone, and with it all their agents. There are no Watchers patrolling the borders of the Church as before, no signs of activity at all. At my insistence, we stay aboveground and outside of the buildings, following the winding pathways to the Grand Regent's tower. If a Black Robe intercepts us, we can, however implausibly, claim that we are simply passersby, curious about the airships we saw hovering overhead earlier. It is unlikely to work, but our guilt will be obvious should we happen to be discovered in one of the tunnels.

I am confident there are none, and my confidence seems well placed as we approach the tower. There we see the only visible remnants of the Society raid: shattered windows on the fifth and sixth floors. Before we enter, we do a loop around the building, exploring the north and west of the campus, just to assure ourselves that it has been abandoned by the Society. When De Vroes is satisfied, we enter the tower and head up the stairs to the second floor.

It appears as though a whirlwind has passed through, with odd bits of clothes and equipment thrown about from the rooms where Osahi's people stayed. The corner where De Vroes kept his equipment has similarly been turned over, but most of it seems to still be there. He looks over everything as Suon and I scout the remainder of the floor, confirming that it is empty. That emptiness is unnerving, the absence of the omnipresent guards speaking for what took place here today. They will now be in Traveler custody, or worse.

"Looks like it's all here," De Vroes says as we return. "Except for the Orb. I'm shocked, frankly."

"Obviously they didn't spend a lot of time here," Suon says. "Looks like everything is here, more or less. Except the people."

"Can you still do it?" I say, looking at Ana.

"I think so," he replies. "The drugs I need are still here. We can improvise a surgical table if need be. There's some other equipment that I can use instead of the Orb. I've had to jury-rig some things since I left the guild."

De Vroes goes to the side room where he stored his equipment to look things over there, while Suon and I look around the room. I am filled with a nervous energy I can't explain, restless and wanting to do something.

"Should we go upstairs and see what happened there?" I say.

Suon shrugs. "De Vroes might need our help."

"There's some things I'd like to get from my room," I say.

Aside from my jacket, there isn't anything there that

I'm aware of. Even it can easily be replaced, though I have no money at hand, which threatens to become a problem if I am forced to find a way to survive in this world without the Church as my foundation. That is not something that can be solved here and certainly not easily. I will have to find my way in the world all over again. The thought leaves me unsettled and I push it aside. For now, I just want to see if Aeida smuggled any other surprises, aside from the hard drive, into our room without my knowing, and to see if the Grand Regent left anything behind that might be of use.

De Vroes returns from the side room with a laptop and some other things in tow. "I think we're good," he says, setting them down. "We'll use that over there for the procedure." He points to an overturned table, and Suon and I retrieve it and set it beside the bench.

"We were thinking of heading upstairs to look around," Suon says.

"That's fine," De Vroes says, already setting things up on the bench. "It will take me half an hour to get set up here."

"You'll be all right?" Suon asks.

De Vroes pats the pulse pistol tucked in his belt in response. I look at Suon and she shrugs. We head to the elevator, with Ana following. My other self stays with De Vroes. I almost turn to tell me to come along, but decide against it. Though I should be keeping a close watch, especially since I am not entirely certain I can trust De Vroes, I cannot bring myself to any longer. Staring at oneself from another body is deeply unnerving, and I have had enough of it today, on top of everything else that has happened.

When the elevator opens on the twelfth floor, I half expect to see Morris there, standing ramrod straight and with a blank expression. The corridor is empty, without even the signs of a struggle that marked the second floor, the doors to the Grand Regent's audience chamber closed.

The hallway is dim with shadows, the only lights coming from the emergency exit sign above the stairwell door. We pause as the elevator doors close behind us, to see if our arrival has come to the attention of anyone who might remain.

The silence that follows is so deep that it begins to seem ominous, and Suon pulls out her pulse weapon. It takes me a moment to realize what is so unnerving about the quiet. None of the usual sounds of a building are present. No hum of electricity from the lights, no movement or air through fans or radiators, no water moving through pipes. Everything but us is still.

"The power's off," Suon says, stating the obvious. "How are the elevators still working?"

"I imagine Molijc made certain this floor was on a different system than the rest of the floors."

"But why kill the power here and not bother with the rest of the building? I mean, the raid was on the sixth floor."

I shake my head. "I don't know. Maybe just an accident. Maybe something else."

I go to my room and conduct a haphazard search. Aeida has left nothing else that I can see. All that I take are my jacket and a cell phone on the night table. I don't recall having it previously, but I assume it was Aeida's. It may be useful. The Society will be able to track it, of course, but the Society doesn't need that to track me. They can find me whenever they want.

After my room, we go through Meredith's and find nothing. It is as I left it before, with only the tangle of sheets to indicate anyone was recently here.

"She certainly knew what was coming," Suon says, staring at the bed. I wonder if she suspects that I was recently in it with Meredith and how that makes her feel.

My own emotions at the sight of the empty bed are overwhelming. I nod, trying to choke back the rising feelings, hoping that nothing is showing on my face. Up until now I have allowed a part of myself to believe that Meredith was caught as unaware as I was by the Traveler raid. She fled without warning me because she couldn't find me and had no time to search. Now, looking at this room again and seeing how scrubbed it is of any trace of Meredith, with nothing for the Society or anyone else to use, doubts flood me.

I stare at the room, trying to recall how it looked the night before, but I had no eyes for those details then. There were clothes on one of the chairs and a few odds and ends on the night table. All gone now. The place has the look and feel of an unused safe house. Did she know the raid was happening when she drew me in here? Was that the plan, to ensure I remained in place for the Society to scoop up?

We leave her quarters and head into the Grand Regent's. The only thing amiss in the audience chamber is the throne, which is sitting askew near the door where the Black Robes shoved it aside. All the stolen antiquities are still in place, untouched, which amazes me. Is this further proof of Molijc's bargain with the Society, or evidence of their purity? It must be the former, for surely their laws must require them to return these objects to their proper universes.

The back rooms are turned over and torn apart, evidence of the Black Robes' attempts to find our hiding place, or to see if anyone else had secreted themselves here. Nothing, so far as I can see, has been removed.

"What will you do? After this?" Suon says quietly as we enter Molijc's quarters.

"I don't know." I glance at her, fingering the hard drive in my pocket. This was where Aeida retrieved it from. I consider returning it to the safe, which still sits in the corner unopened. What need do I have for it anymore? There is only the past there, and all those old battles I cannot bring myself to care about anymore. But I decide against it. Aeida must have retrieved it for a reason, and I am curious to discover what that was.

"It will depend on Ana," I say, looking in her direction. She looks at me blankly, a half-smile on her face at the sound of her name.

"Why her?" Suon says, working hard to keep the jealousy from her voice.

"It's not like that," I say, turning away from Ana. It is difficult still to see her like this, almost as difficult as looking at my half-self. They are reminders of all my failures, all the wrong done in my name. "I owe her. It's my fault she's in this situation. I have to try to get her out. Maybe she tells me to fuck off, that she never wants to see me again. That's what I would do. But if she asks for my help, I have to give it."

Suon is quiet, clearly miserable, wanting to say something but not knowing how. "But what about after all of this? What then?"

I let out a bitter laugh as I go over to the safe and study the dial, wondering if the combination is the same. It must be if Aeida was able to get it open. He could only have gotten the combination from my memories. How he did so is a disconcerting question. Is he lurking behind my thoughts, even now?

I look up at Suon, who will not meet my eyes. "Will I run away with you? Is that what you want to know?" I shake my head. "If I'm being honest, I don't think this will ever be over. I can't see past it."

"It will, if you want it to be. You have to choose it." Suon looks at me, her expression earnest and pleading.

"Oh, it's that easy, is it? You haven't been in this like I have. You think the Society will let me walk away? The Seekers? Molijc? No chance. They will never. I know too much."

"What do you have that they want? Molijc is a double agent. I know you don't believe that, but he is." Suon waves a hand in an angry gesture. "And the Society and Seekers have what they want. The Church is broken.

Without you, Lasinha, or Osahi, what's left? Nothing."

I am not so certain as she that I have nothing the Seekers or the Travelers want, recalling what the Seeker told me of a battle within the Society. Whatever the truth of that, and I am not sure how much I credit anything he told me, he will find me again. Of that much I am certain. So long as he thinks I can be a pawn in whatever game he is playing.

I don't mention him to Suon. "The Watchers are still out there, and the Acolytes. There are still enough faithful to have a Church. The Regents and sub-Regents who are left now will never leave. They're committed absolutely. None of them will believe Molijc is working with the Society. Even I can't, really. Whatever the game is they're all playing, they will all see me as a threat."

"Not if you go. Not if you renounce the faith and go."

"They won't let me," I say, trying the combination to the safe. "They can't conceive of someone like me walking away from this. They'll think it's another play."

The door to the safe swings open, and I give a low whistle as I see what is inside. Suon and Ana both come over to see what I have found.

"Holy shit," Suon says. "It's a fortune. Why didn't he take this?"

"No time, maybe. The real question is why the Travelers didn't." I begin to leaf through the stacks of bills, pulling out those that are from this universe. There is close to thirty thousand by my quick count.

"They cut a deal with Molijc."

"So it would seem," I say, pocketing half the bills and handing the rest to Suon. "We'll divide it three ways between us."

She frowns, about to offer some protest, but is stopped short by a loud ringtone, a calypso version of "Tangled Up in Blue." We stare at each other until I recall the cell phone I picked up in my quarters. I search my pockets and find it at last in my jacket, which I threw on Molijc's bed while I was going through the safe. The number on the display is a local one, but otherwise I can tell nothing about who is calling.

With another glance at Suon, and a resigned shrug, I answer it.

"Laila," Meredith says, her relief apparent in her voice. "I'm so glad you found this."

"Laila," Meredith says again when I don't reply immediately. "Are you alone?"

"More or less," I say, looking at Suon, who takes my hint and nods.

Meredith laughs. It is a relieved laugh, with an undercurrent of nervousness. "You found yourself, did you? That's good. I'm glad you made it out. I was worried."

"Are you alone?" I say.

"Yes," she says without hesitation. The nervousness is gone from her voice, which puts me more on edge. It means she expected the question and has prepared her answer. "How did you get out? I'm sorry. I didn't know where you were, and when I saw the airships, I didn't think I had much time."

"It all worked out," I say. "I still know a few things about the campus that the Society doesn't."

She laughs. "I suppose you do." A pause, where I can hear her swallow. "Where are you now?"

"Nearby," I say, refusing to elaborate. I will give her nothing until I know for certain where she stands.

If she is with the Watchers right now, or the Society,

205

for that matter, they will be able to track me using the phone, which may be why she left it for me to find. Or perhaps she left it when she couldn't find me, hoping I would find it and she could contact me. That seems too great a risk to take. If the Society found it, she would risk revealing her position to them, unless she has taken other precautions. Why chance that kind of exposure?

As if she is following my thoughts, Meredith says, "It was risky leaving behind the phone, but I couldn't think of any other way to get in contact with you."

Another pause to gauge my reaction. I say nothing, forcing her to do the work, letting her know that she needs to persuade me. Suon is watching me through narrowed eyes, clearly agitated and wanting me to end the call now. She is probably right, but I don't. I will give Meredith this one chance—how many last chances is this?—to convince me that she has not betrayed me again.

"I understand why you're suspicious," Meredith says.

"I'm not. I know exactly what happened here today." Of course, I don't, but I want to gauge her reaction.

Another pause. "You're wrong. I swear to you. I'm trying to set things right, just like I said. The raid was just bad luck."

"For Osahi. Who were you talking to the other night? Who were you supposed to keep in play? It was me, wasn't it? That's what you were doing last night, making sure I didn't go anywhere."

"Think about what you're saying," Meredith says, irritated. "Why would I want you captured by the Society?"

"You tell me."

"Look, I didn't know the raid was coming until I saw the airships outside my window. I checked your room, but you weren't there, so I had to go. I'm not about to be disappeared to some Society black site."

"Indeed. Who were you talking to the other night?"

"I don't have time to explain everything, Laila. Not now. I have to keep moving. You should too. The

Travelers aren't going to be satisfied with just Osahi. They're going to want more. I can help you."

It is my turn to pause. "And what sort of help would that be, Meredith? The kind that comes with me waking up in a new body with no idea who I am?"

The hurt I hear in her voice is real. "You know that wasn't my choice. That was between him and you. None of this has been my choice. But I meant what I said. I want to set this right. If you give me a chance, I will. I want what we had before, Laila. I know you do too. I can see it in your eyes."

I want what she says to be true. The emotion in her voice pulls at me, even as I know that she isn't telling me the truth. At least not all of it.

"You're right," I say. "That's what I want. What about your Acolyte?"

Another pause. "I haven't reached him yet, but he'll restore you."

"He has the equipment?"

"He can get it. Just tell me where you are and we can find a place to rendezvous and figure out our next steps."

"Ana is part of the deal too," I say. "She gets restored or I walk away."

The pause this time is the longest of all. "She's with you?" I don't respond. "Okay. I think he'll do that too, but I can't promise. The Acolytes have never trusted the Arajuanos."

I don't say anything, motioning to Suon and Ana that we should head for the elevator. We make our way through the Grand Regent's chambers out to the audience room.

"Are you near the campus?" Meredith says. "We could try to meet somewhere near there. I know a safe house we can go to."

"After today, are you sure of any safe houses? I can't imagine the campus is safe either. The Society must still have people there."

Meredith dismisses this breezily: "I don't think so. It would bring too much attention to what they're doing."

"I think the raid did that already."

"More attention, then." Meredith pauses yet again. This time I can almost hear her thinking about what she should say to get me to do what she wants. "Why don't we try to meet on the north side of the campus? Right at Thirty-seventh and Thirty-second. You and Ana can just be a couple out for a stroll for the evening. I'll come pick you up. How soon can you be there?"

The elevator we came in still stands open. The three of us get in and I press the button for the second floor. The doors hiss close, and I wonder if Meredith can hear them. The intersection where she wants me to go is right on the northern border of the campus. It is also the point where one of the tunnels emerges, after an extension that was built before my exile. Meredith must know, or at least suspect, I am somewhere near the campus, and she is hoping I will use the tunnels to get to that intersection.

"That's a little too close to campus for my comfort. What if the Travelers see us? They know Ana. They may even know me."

"You know how to get there without them noticing," Meredith says, sounding exasperated. Underneath her irritation, I can hear a hint of nervousness, a twinge in her voice that suggests she knows she is failing to convince me. "Just let me know when you can get there and I will be there with a vehicle. You won't even be on the street long enough for anyone to notice."

"I doubt that very much," I say as the elevator doors open and I step out onto the second floor, followed by Suon and Ana. "Who'll be waiting for me there? The same person you were talking with the other night?"

There is no answer from Meredith. I glance over at Suon, who is watching me pensively, her lips moving silently, as though she is only barely holding in her thoughts.

"I see," I say. "Goodbye, Meredith. Tell Molijc I have the files."

Before she can say anything in response, I hang up the phone and toss it into the elevator. I press the button for the twelfth floor, step out, and let the doors close and the elevator rise.

"We need to get moving," I say, turning back to Suon. "No time for De Vroes to work his magic. Someone will be here soon."

Suon nods, and we make our way from the elevator banks toward the corner where we left De Vroes and myself. Neither of them is visible as we emerge from the corridor into the open area where Osahi established his stronghold. I stop in my tracks and reach into my belt to pull out my pulse weapon. Beside me, Suon does the same. I have the same sense of something being terribly amiss as I did in the moments before she and De Vroes arrived on the twelfth floor right before the Black Robes did.

A scan of the floor reveals nothing. Ana lurks behind me, and I consider sending her back down the corridor to the elevators, but I don't know if that will be safer for her. I look at Suon, and she gestures her intent to go forward.

"I'll cover you," I say under my breath.

Before Suon can move, De Vroes emerges from one of the side rooms where Osahi's people were encamped. He moves stiffly, his expression grim and strained, his hands held up as though he wants to tell us to be quiet. As he comes nearer, Osahi steps from behind him, keeping his pulse pistol leveled at the Acolyte's head.

"Drop your weapons," he says, jerking his head in our direction.

I ignore him and look at De Vroes. "Where is my body?"

De Vroes shakes his head. "I'm sorry," he says in a low voice.

"Drop your weapons," Osahi says, trying to look menacing.

209

He sounds crazed and strikes a pathetic figure, his finely tailored shirt in disarray, his powder-blue jacket nowhere to be seen. How did he manage to escape the Black Robes and why did they not remain to capture him? His defeated posture and the ruins of all he worked for that lie around us provide an answer of sorts.

Suon lowers her weapon, uncertain of what to do, but I keep mine trained upon Osahi, not flinching. "You fucking bastard," I say, surprised at the lack of emotion in my voice. Within there is a surge of turmoil that wrenches my stomach, followed by nothing, a flatness of emotion, my entire being homing in on the man who may have ended any hope I have of returning to my body.

Osahi laughs. "You deserve it. You're a traitor to the faith. Even now you're trying to restore this Traveler agent. You've always been a fool for her, and look what it has gotten you."

"Speaking of fools," I say in a grim voice, nodding at the refuse that lies around us. "Molijc wasn't quite the fool he appeared, was he?"

"He is exactly what he always appeared," Osahi says in a haughty voice that would be laughable were he not holding a gun.

"He betrayed the Church to the Society. Not Ana," Suon says, unable to contain herself any longer.

"Molijc is a puppet, nothing more. This one," Osahi says, pointing his pistol at De Vroes, who winces at the gesture. "His kind are the true rulers of the faith, make no mistake of it. If you're looking for who sold out the faith to the Society, look no further. They sent me this snake to convince me that the Acolytes could be my allies and were to be reasoned with, and what was the result? All my people are disappeared to black sites."

"I had nothing to do with that," De Vroes says through clenched teeth. "I warned you."

"Don't you start. Shut your mouth." Osahi shakes his gun at De Vroes, nearly in tears. He is deeply unstable, something in him broken by the events of the day, which makes him dangerous.

"Let's all put down our guns, Osahi," I say. "We're all on the same side here. None of us want Molijc in charge of the faith. We all want the Acolytes stopped. The Society too. So let's just talk and see what we can do next."

Osahi laughs wildly and for far too long. "Don't you understand? Molijc is not in charge of the faith. The Acolytes are. They've cut their deal with the Society. The Church will go forward with Molijc as its puppet, and they will get to perfect their work without any Traveler interference. They've never believed. This is what they want." He points at me and at Ana. "They've got you out of the way. Probably Lasinha too. Molijc is utterly deluded. And today they dealt with me. Who is left to oppose them?"

"We are," I say, though I no more believe it than him. "So long as we're free, we can oppose what they're doing to the faith."

Osahi shakes his head, as though I am a naïve child who does not understand the ways of the world. "The Society left us for the Watchers. We can run, but where to? Molijc and Lasinha destroyed your network. Mine is gone now too. Because of you."

His lips curl viciously and he smashes the butt of his pistol against the back of De Vroes' head. The Acolyte grunts and stumbles to the floor.

"You were the one who encouraged this alliance with Molijc. Who said that I could use it to convince the Acolytes and the Order that I was the safer bet. They pretended to listen, but they never had any intention of making me Grand Regent. They were just stringing me along. Just like you."

Osahi is not even looking at the rest of us, leaning over De Vroes, who holds his hands up to shield himself from further blows.

"That's not true," Suon says, ignoring a sharp look

from me. "He warned you about the Acolytes. He told you they weren't to be trusted. He knew. But you wouldn't listen."

Osahi pays no attention to her. "Do you deny it?" he shouts again and again at De Vroes, punctuating each one with a jab of his pistol. The Acolyte does not answer, still holding his hands up.

I watch all this, unsure what to do. "Osahi," I say, in a loud voice that I want to be commanding but instead sounds scared. "Forget him. There are faithful who will join us. We can build the Church again."

He looks at me, the pistol still pointed down at De Vroes. "Don't you get it, Laila? There are no faithful left. The Acolytes have seen to that."

He pulls the trigger, and De Vroes convulses and goes still. Suon screams and Osahi turns his gun on her, a snarl twisting his face. I am certain he is going to shoot her. Before he does, his face goes blank and he falls, his gun clattering to the floor beside him. I go to stand over him, my gun still aimed at him, waiting to see if he is still able to get to his feet. But Osahi is still, his chest not even moving.

I turn to Suon, who holds up her hands, her face twisted in fear. "Please put the gun down, Laila."

I am surprised to see it still in my hand, still pointing in her direction. But I do not lower it. Someone shot Osahi and I have to stay ready.

"Please put the gun down, Laila. It is you, isn't it?" Suon takes a tentative step in my direction, flinching as my hand tightens on the pistol. "It's okay. It's over."

"Someone shot him," I say, scanning the room for any movement.

"You did, Laila. Put the gun down. Please. We have to see if they're okay."

I look at Suon, not quite trusting what she is saying. But at last the unnatural quiet of the room, where the shadows are growing deeper as the sun begins to set, convinces me of what she is saying. I lower my weapon and return it to my belt, while Suon lets out a relieved sigh. She rushes to check the two fallen men, feeling for their pulses. I watch, distant somehow from the entire scene, as though this were all happening to someone else. It is—my own body is elsewhere, likely dead.

"He's dead," Suon says, looking up from De Vroes, crestfallen. "Osahi still has a pulse, but it's weak."

Suon stands up and looks at me warily. "Is everything all right, Laila?" I blink and nod, but this does not seem to reassure her. "Okay. Let's go look for your body."

I nod again, though I want to say there is no point. If De Vroes is dead, it means Osahi's weapon was not set to stun, and my body, and whatever was within it, is dead as well. Still I follow Suon as she goes to the room that De Vroes and Osahi emerged from. Ana walks beside me, almost protectively, I think, and I look at her. Her expressions seem similar to my own feeling, vacant and absent, with a faraway gaze.

My body lies sprawled in the room the two men came from, amidst various pieces of equipment and supplies scattered on the floor. Suon rushes to it, and I watch distractedly as she checks my body for signs of life.

"There's still a pulse. Barely," Suon says, looking up at me. I frown, uncertain how I am supposed to be receiving this news. "She's breathing, too. Osahi must have shot her from quite far."

Suon stares at me for a moment and then, receiving no reaction from me, gets up and heads back into the main room. Ana and I watch her go, neither of us stirring. Suon returns several minutes later, her hands full with various bottles of Acolyte drugs from De Vroes' shelves. She sets them down beside my body, selects one, and fills a syringe with it and injects my body.

I observe no immediate change, but Suon seems satisfied. She digs through the room until she finds a bag in one corner and fills it with the drugs she collected, as well as several packages of syringes that she finds. When she is done, she zips it up and throws it over her shoulder. She looks at me and sighs.

"Laila," she says in a gentle voice, "we have to go now."

My instinct is to refuse, but I simply do not respond. I don't trust her, and I cannot seem to get a firm grasp on what is going on right now.

"Whoever Meredith is sending is coming soon. We can't stay." Suon reaches out to take my hand, but I flinch and step backward. The look on her face is heartbreaking, yet I feel nothing.

I turn and look down at my body and back at Suon. She looks at me, tears in her eyes, and says in a choking voice, "We have to go, Laila. You have to come with me now."

I look at her, uncomprehending. Ana puts a comforting hand on my shoulder and I look at her. There is nothing to see in her expression, but it awakens something in me. We go to my body and pick it up, carrying it, one of us under each arm. Suon watches this with a grieving expression, but she says nothing. When we are ready, she leads us away, out of the tower and off the campus.

EXCERPT:

THE SOJOURNER
VOLUME FIVE OF
THE SOJOURNERS CYCLE

Laila's strange and reluctant alliance with the Seeker continues, though she does not know where it will lead her. She fears it will place her in another prison, worse than the one she has just managed to escape.

But her escape is not entirely complete. For though she has been restored to her own flesh, parts of Aeida somehow still remain. Along with some other she does not recognize. Is this some aftereffect of the Acolyte's bizarre procedure? Or the result of the Seeker's meddling?

All this pales in comparison to what Laila soon discovers. That she has an unwanted part to play in an ancient struggle for who will rule the crossings between the universes and all that lies in them.

In the stunning conclusion to the Sojourners Cycle Laila will be faced with a terrible choice, one that will decide her fate and humanity's.

1

The sound of birds chirping outside my window awakens me. Sparrows or swallows, or some other tiny, dull species that covers the globe in endless numbers. I sit up carefully, having made the mistake earlier in my stay of forgetting how close the ceiling is to the loft bed. Several painful mistakes actually. But then I am always forgetting where I am. It takes effort to remember, to fight through whatever happens to me when I sleep.

At least I am certain of who I am. That part of me remains stable. Aeida is gone. Suon assures me I have not taken to wandering and plotting in the night. I trust her, as far as that goes.

It seems she did not betray me when I was with her at Osahi's fortress and she was not lying when she said she loved me. She does, though I cannot fathom why. I am a lost and broken soul in a foreign body. A pitiful thing who has done terrible deeds. The evidence of my failures is still with us: Ana and my self. It is Ana's presence that provides the window to allow me to finally see the truth of Suon's feelings for me. She is jealous of Ana and how much I care for her.

Envious that we share a bed, though that is at Ana's

insistence not mine. It makes me uncomfortable, especially with the always-present threat that Aeida may return. There is no doubt of what he would do to her, given the chance. I have experienced it, and that is not something I can forget. Or forgive myself for. But there is so much that is unforgivable in my past that it is hard to know where to begin with an accounting, let alone trying to set it right.

I have decided I will begin with Ana, though I have no means to help her and no idea how to go about acquiring them. That is not entirely true. The Seeker would be able to help her and would perhaps even be willing. She was a Society agent after all. At least for a time. More importantly, I am one now, ostensibly, though I have done nothing for them. That is another accounting I will have to face soon, and it amazes me I haven't yet.

Where is the Seeker? Why hasn't he come to see that I make good on what I promised him? For that matter, I don't understand why the Society didn't remain at the Church campus after their raid until they had driven me to ground. Surely, having destroyed the Church, they have no need for me to do the same. Molijc was the one who did the destroying, but it seems he was working for them too. I cannot believe that was always the case. My mind refuses to contemplate it. My life cannot be more of a lie than it already is.

The question of when the Seeker or the Society will descend to seize me is just another specter that clings to me, along with the threat of Aeida's return, haunting every hour of every day. I expect to spend however much time remains to me trapped in this false body on the run from those who wish to destroy me, or locked away and forgotten in some cell. If Aeida were to somehow manage to return and banish me to the void again it would almost be a relief.

I swing my legs so that I am sitting on the edge of the bed, looking down on the rest of the house. Ana stirs but does not wake beside me. I decide I should get up before I disturb her further, and walk, back bent, to the ladder and descend from the loft as quietly as I can manage. The door to Suon's room is beside the ladder, and though it is closed I suspect she is already awake. She has trouble sleeping. I have different problems.

We are staying in a ski lodge in the mountains several hours west of Calgary near a town called Golden. Once it was a resort town, but now, like so much else in this world, it has fallen into disrepair. There are few people left in Calgary and not many are able to head out to the mountains to ski or hike, and those that do stay closer to Calgary. As a result, the town here has been mostly forgotten, with a few dozen inhabitants left. One of them runs the lodges here, halfway up the mountain from the town. We are his only guests and have been since we arrived almost a month ago.

I start the coffee maker and sit at the kitchen table to watch it drip into the pot. As I expected, Suon is awake and she emerges when the pot is almost full. We have our routines now.

"How was your sleep?" she says in a faux cheerful voice.

I glare at her. "I dreamed again."

"Do you remember any of it?" Suon gets up to pour us both coffee.

I shake my head as I watch her spoon sugar into my cup. In my old body I preferred coffee with milk and sugar, but in Aeida's I drink my coffee black.

"Really?" she says. It is a challenge. She does not believe me.

"Really," I say, which is a lie. I remember the dreams clearly, even if I would rather forget them.

Suon takes the hint and decides to leave matters be. She pulls a box cereal from the cupboard and pours herself a bowl. "We're out of milk," she says, when she goes to the fridge and returns to the kitchen table to eat her cereal dry.

I listen to the crunch of her chewing, staring out the window at the tree-covered mountainside, taking nothing in and trying not to think of anything at all. Suon is watching me as she eats—I can sense her gaze—working her way up to ask me another question. Already I know what it will be.

"We need to go into town for groceries," she says. "At least one of us does."

I make a noncommittal noise, not turning from my scrutiny of the mountain.

Suon waits, and when I do not reply, says, "I think you should go. You haven't really left the lodge since we got here."

I don't bother to say anything in response. We have variations of the same conversation every day. It always ends the same way. This discussion will too.

"How long are we planning on staying here?" Suon says.

The question surprises me a little. She hasn't asked it in so long. "Depends," I say.

"We can't stay here forever."

"With the money I have I can stay here for at least a year," I say.

"And what then?"

I sip my coffee, still not looking at her. She does not want to hear what I have to say. I am just waiting for the Seeker, the Society, or the Church to find me. Someone will eventually, no matter where I go. There seems no point in running or trying to hide, when it will end the same regardless. In this body I can be found anywhere in this universe.

"No one's asking you to stay here," I say.

Suon does not reply and when I finally look over I see she is weeping.

THE SOJOURNER will be available in November 2018.

ABOUT THE AUTHOR

Clint Westgard is the author of The Shadow Men Trilogy and the science fiction epic The Sojourners Cycle. In addition, he has published a work of historical fantasy set in colonial Peru, The Maleficio Chronicles, and a retelling of the Minotaur legend, The Trials of the Minotaur. Clint Westgard lives in Calgary, Alberta.

ALSO BY CLINT WESTGARD

The Sojourner
Volume Five of The Sojourners Cycle

Laila's strange and reluctant alliance with the Seeker
continues, though she does not know where it will lead
her. She fears it will place her in another prison, worse
than the one she has just managed to escape.

But her escape is not entirely complete. For though she
has been restored to her own flesh, parts of Aeida
somehow still remain. Along with some other she does not
recognize. Is this some aftereffect of the Acolyte's bizarre
procedure? Or the result of the Seeker's meddling?

All this pales in comparison to what Laila soon discovers.
That she has an unwanted part to play in an ancient
struggle for who will rule the crossings between the
universes and all that lies in them.

In the stunning conclusion to the Sojourners Cycle Laila
will be faced with a terrible choice, one that will decide her
fate and humanity's.

ALSO BY CLINT WESTGARD

Realm of Shadows
Volume One of The Shadow Men
An Alkemya Novel

Craitol and Renuih, two empires a world apart, divided by the desert that lies between them. A desert ruled by the Shadow Men.

An uneasy peace holds sway in both realms, hiding longstanding feuds and bitter rivalries. Until a Shadow Men raid on Renuih shatters the calm and sets in motion events no one can control.

Masiph id Ezern, unfavored son of the Imperial Vazeir, finds himself a hero following the raid. His father remains unmoved by his exploits and, in his bitterness, Masiph will find himself a reluctant participant in a plot against the empire.

As he finds himself drawn deeper and deeper into the conspiracy, he soon realizes there will be no escaping the realm of shadows, where intrigue and betrayal abound. And though the Shadow Men have gone quiet, they will not stay silent forever…

ALSO BY CLINT WESTGARD

Council of Shadows
Volume Two of The Shadow Men
An Alkemya Novel

Discontent continues to fester within the realms of Craitol and Renuih, fed by intrigues carried out in the shadows. As rivals and apostates struggle for supremacy, a long incubated plan begins to unfold.

Vyissan, a mysterious alkemycal practitioner arrives in Renuih, the latest strike in a long war over who shall control the secrets of alkemya and Craitol itself. He carries with him a secret that, once revealed, will reverberate across all realms. Before he can reveal it though, the conspirators against the emperor will strike their own blow.

But now, a new and more powerful menace looms on the horizon. The Shadow Men have gained the secrets of the Council Adept's alkemya and no one can be certain what they will do with it…

ALSO BY CLINT WESTGARD

Dance of Shadows
Volume Three of The Shadow Men
An Alkemya Novel

War with the Shadow Men looms in both realms as the consequences of the Gvers' Council in Craitol begin to make themselves known. A war that could end in glorious triumph or bitter disaster.

Doubt shadows everyone's steps, for they know there are no certainties in the desert. Especially now the Shadow Men have made the art of alkemya their own.

No one has more questions than Vyissan, for he is working in service to a cause he is no longer sure he believes in. And now he must undertake a journey with those who both loathe and fear him. Before the first sword is drawn, his life will be under threat.

But his will not be the only one, for somewhere in the desert the Shadow Men lie in wait…

ALSO BY CLINT WESTGARD

Unspeakable Rites
An Alkemya Novella

A dead man of no family or account is what Gahryll, Chief
Magister of Tson, sees when the corpse of an Enir youth is
brought to the Magisterium. But Magister Mihuibel sees
something else: a conspiracy involving false adepts
practicing an outlawed form of alkemya.

Against his better instincts Gahryll authorizes an
investigation that draws both Magisters into the seamy
underbelly of Tson where the rich and powerful prey upon
the desperate. When the inquiry implicates one of the most
important families in the Realm of Craitol in forbidden
practices and false alkemya, their positions and ranks will
be threatened.

But that is only the beginning. For the killer will stop at
nothing to ensure his secrets remain hidden and Gahryll is
brought face to face with the unspeakable power of
alkemya that has been unleashed. It forces him to make a
choice. Will he risk everything to fight for justice in a
realm ruled where rank and wealth are all that matter?

Set in the same universe as The Shadow Men Trilogy,
Unspeakable Rites, further explores the nature of alkemya,
its terrible power, and the heavy price paid for its use.

ALSO BY CLINT WESTGARD

The Maleficio Chronicles

Luisa is always more than she appears. Rumor and mystery surround her. And strange events seem to follow wherever she goes.

Born in Lima, City of Kings, to a noble family, her father so fears her true nature that he banishes her to a convent. There she falls under the suspicion of the Inquisition and decides to flee.

Disguised as a man, she embarks upon a series of wild adventures, dueling, carousing, and gambling her way across colonial Peru. But everything changes when someone recognizes her for what she truly is, and soon she finds herself fighting for her very survival.

In a world where she will always stand apart, Luisa undergoes a strange journey, marked by betrayal and murder, terrible powers and mysterious strangers. *The Maleficio Chronicles* is her incredible confession and a story like no other.

ALSO BY CLINT WESTGARD

The Trials of the Minotaur

In the fifth year of the rule of Auten the One Eyed a minotaur is born to one of Colosi's most important families.

Taken from his mother as a newborn, exiled and cast from his family, the minotaur vows to return to the imperial city and take his rightful place as a patrician in the empire. But the patriarch of the family, his grandfather, will stop at nothing to see this blemish to his honor destroyed.

And so begins an epic journey, through lands beyond imagining, marked by despair and exile, triumph and betrayal. At its heart lies a quest to be free.